MEDICINE FEATHER

Prospectors in the hills are being ambushed and killed by a gang determined to snatch every ounce of gold that is dug from the ground or panned from the streams. But when one such attack earns the robbers nothing but a pack of pelts, it sets in motion a chain of events leading to a bloody conclusion. For the victim — Medicine Feather, brother of the Arapaho and friend of the Sioux — is unwilling to relinquish his possessions without seeking revenge . . .

WILL DUREY

MEDICINE
FEATHER

Complete and Unabridged

LINFORD
Leicester

First published in Great Britain in 2014 by
Robert Hale Limited
London

First Linford Edition
published 2016
by arrangement with
Robert Hale
an imprint of The Crowood Press
Wiltshire

A catalogue record for this book is available
from the British Library.

ISBN 978–1–4448–3077–4

Published by
F. A. Thorpe (Publishing)
Anstey, Leicestershire

Set by Words & Graphics Ltd.
Anstey, Leicestershire
Printed and bound in Great Britain by
T. J. International Ltd., Padstow, Cornwall

This book is printed on acid-free paper

1

From his youth, with neither place to call home nor folks to call family, Weston Gray had travelled the uncharted country west of the Missouri, living the arduous life of a trapper and earning a paltry living from the pelts he sold, but by the time he was twenty-five, due to his association with the last of the mountain men and the tribespeople through whose land he wandered, he had gained such knowledge of the country as few others possessed. He had crossed prairie land, climbed mountains, dwelt in forests and navigated rivers whose existence were known to few other white men.

Sometimes he would make a temporary home with a tribe of Sioux or Arapaho people, joining in their summer hunt or sharing their winter deprivations and learning that their primitive lifestyle required an understanding of their role in the natural world, how they affected and were affected by their surroundings and the seasons. Wes was a quick learner, soon able to predict changes in the weather as easily as he could identify the best types of rock for making arrowheads, tools and weapons. The tribesmen taught him their language, both their spoken tongue and the sign language common to all the tribes that wandered the Plains. In addition, he soon came to recognize the habits of other creatures and how to interpret the message in any abnormal behaviour, and, too, he became aware of those plants and trees which bore fruit he could eat, or had seeds, leaves, roots or sap which he could crush and pulverize for medicinal purposes.

He fought the enemies of those he chose to live among, danced at their ceremonies and told tales around their fires until he became accepted by the elders and was allowed to speak as an equal at their village council. The Sioux called him *Wiyaka Wakan*, which is Medicine Feather, and on more than one occasion he spoke on their behalf at treaty meetings with the American military. Among the nomadic tribes of the Plains, Medicine Feather became a name as much feared as it was honoured, while that of Wes Gray aroused similar emotions among the white Americans.

After the War Between the States, Wes's knowledge of the land west of the Missouri prompted his friend, Major Caleb Dodge, to hire him as chief scout for the wagon train he was leading to California. Such a journey appealed to Wes and each year after that he and Caleb led settlers west, either to California or Oregon.

Wes established an annual routine, one which was almost as fixed as a grizzly's need for winter sleep or the springtime return of the grey goose to the valleys along the upper Missouri.

The journey west extended from late spring to late autumn, and when it was completed he'd make his way to the Wind River country, to the Arapaho village which was the winter home of his wife, Little Feather, and there he'd spend the cold months trapping beaver whose pelts he would sell when he returned east.

In spring, when the days warmed and the tribe moved towards the buffalo trails, Wes went with them, the first stage in returning to the towns of his own people where the next wagon train would be assembling. When their summer village was established he would pack his pelts into a canoe and continue his journey alone, following the tributaries that led him on to the great Missouri and onward to Council Bluffs. With the rivers in full flood he was able to complete the journey in less than half the time it would take on horseback.

Wes was accustomed to travelling alone. Even when he was guiding wagons westward he was scarcely with them, instead scouting ahead for unexpected hazards or hunting for fresh meat. For him, the long river journey was an opportunity to test his abilities against nature, to use the power of the great water flow to speed him to his destination. He had travelled the course many times and knew that for most of the journey there was little to fear, his main task merely to keep the canoe straight and let the current carry him forward.

Those parts of the river that were less friendly were well known to him. Some stretches of white water he tackled with confidence, remembering a course that would avoid any rocks that were capable of ripping the bottom from the canoe, but others he would treat with greater respect, leaving the watercourse and carrying his boat and goods to a point downstream where it was safe to re-enter the water. The last of those natural obstacles occurred almost forty miles short of his destination, a double impediment both aspects of which required him to get off the river. The first was 200 yards of rock-strewn rapids followed, just a mile further downstream, by a drop of more than thirty feet. It was about noon when he approached the rapids, steered to the right-hand bank and pulled the light canoe from the water. The riverbank was lush with spring grass and the dense trees behind were heavy with their new leaves. The smell of blossom filled the air and patches of bright colour decorated the waterside bushes. There was a slight breeze but the high sun was too strong for it to have a chilling effect. Wes ate some of the pemmican that Little Feather had wrapped in doeskin for his journey. One small cake of the dried buffalo meat and grain remained, which was all he needed as he would be in Council Bluffs in two days. On the journey, he'd supplemented her supplies with fresh fish and rabbit for his evening meal, but the small cakes of pemmican were ideal sustenance which could be eaten without breaking his journey.

He toted his small sack of belongings and pack of pelts 400 yards downstream, deposited them, then returned for the canoe. The small craft was light enough to carry on his back and he had got it halfway to the spot where he'd left his belongings when he became aware of a change in the birdsong. The sandpipers and kingfishers still fished at the riverside but the buntings, flickers and orioles had fallen silent among the trees high above the river. After unloading the canoe Wes scanned the wooded slopes, but the multitude of trees made it impossible for anything to be seen. Eventually he attributed the stillness and the silence in the upper reaches of the hillside to a large predator, a grizzly bear or an elk rummaging for food.

After resettling his possessions in the canoe he prepared to push it back into the river. Suddenly, responding to an inexplicable sensation of being watched, Wes turned once again to scan the hillside. For a moment there seemed to be some movement there, off to his left, downstream of where he stood, but just as quickly it was gone, suggesting he'd glimpsed nothing more than the brief flight of a yellow-tailed flicker. In a while, when the sounds of the forest returned to normal, Wes paddled out to the middle of the stream.

A few minutes later he could see the approaching drop and when he got within a hundred yards he began to feel the stronger pull of the current. Now was the time to leave the river. Past experience had taught him that, once ashore, the left-hand bank provided the easier descent to the base of the falls, but looking ahead he could see that his usual landing spot was obstructed by a collection of timbers and debris swept downstream on the flood. Driving the paddle into the water in an attempt to slow his progress, Wes scanned ahead for another beaching site but nothing was immediately obvious. Now the water's edge appeared to be dominated by boulders, which were having the effect of narrowing the river and consequently increasing its momentum towards the cascade. The canoe swept on for another twenty yards and Wes knew that he had to beach her soon.

He looked across to the other bank where a small inlet seemed to offer him a haven, but before he was able to change course to reach it a thick rope suddenly rose from the water ahead, forming a thin barrier across the river. The unexpected obstruction combined with the fierce flow of the river gave Wes no time in which to react. The rope caught him across the chest, cartwheeling him over the back of the canoe and into the water.

The first thing he realized when he broke the surface of the water was that the current had swept his small craft well beyond his reach. It had twisted in its progress towards the waterfall, was almost square-on as it reached the lip and would undoubtedly be destroyed when it went over the top. Self-preservation was uppermost in Wes's mind but even as he kicked powerfully for the left-hand bank his mind was filled with the knowledge that putting him in the river had been a deliberate act. Above the sound of the river he could hear men's voices calling from the far bank.

Despite the fact that his heavy buckskin clothing was proving cumbersome in the water, he was making progress towards the less turbulent side waters. He threw a look towards the far bank and saw that there were three men shouting and gesticulating in his direction. He couldn't believe they were calls of encouragement because they had to be the men responsible for putting his life in danger. When he reached the collection of timbers where he had originally hoped to beach his canoe, he learned the purpose behind their shouts. A fourth man emerged from the pile of timber and loomed over Wes as he attempted to drag himself from the river. In his hands he held a stout pole, perhaps six feet long, which, without ceremony, he swung at Wes's head.

Instinctively, Wes dropped back under the water and the swipe missed him completely, but his assailant wasn't discouraged by this first setback. He took another swing when Wes raised his head again, only to achieve the same result. However, as a means of pulling himself out of the water, Wes grabbed one of the bottom timbers, and in so doing provided another target for his opponent. The man slashed downwards, intending to crush Wes's hand, but the blow was deflected when it struck an outcropping timber. The impetus unbalanced the man. He still held on to the pole but the bottom end slid into the water. Wes saw an opportunity, grabbed and jerked it roughly, completely unbalancing the man, who fell into the river with a yell.

They grappled, the man clinging

tenaciously to the pole as a weapon, spluttering out water but desperately seeking an opportunity to make another strike at Wes's head. But Wes was no stranger to brawling and knew that he had to keep close to his opponent to prevent a full swing of his arms. Wes tried to land a blow to the other's stomach but it was blocked and he was pushed further into the river. The fast-flowing water separated them.

More shouts came from across the water but Wes paid them no heed. The man before him was his immediate concern. Still holding the pole, the man swung it once more at Wes's head, but the current was dragging at him, pulling him downstream. Wes went under the water and, as he did so, drew from its sheath the knife he carried at his waist. Before understanding Wes's intention or even realizing that he was armed, the man was dead. Without breaking the surface of the water Wes swam forward and lunged at his enemy, thrusting the blade of the Bowie knife between the man's ribs. Wes had no compunction about killing the man. The fight had not been of his making and it had clearly been a case of kill or be killed. He held on to the body and together they drifted under water for a short distance until the edge of the waterfall was just a few yards ahead.

Replacing his knife, Wes looked across to the far bank. The threesome had moved, were now heading downstream, taking the route down to the foot of the falls, where his destroyed canoe would, by now, have shed its load. It wasn't clear to Wes whether they had witnessed the end of the fight, or knew that their comrade was dead, but no one had hung around to help him. Wes released the body, allowing the river to take it while he kicked out on his own for the river-bank. His efforts were still being hampered by his long buckskin jacket and he knew he had to rid himself of it if he was going to gain the safety of the bank, but to get his arms out of the sleeves meant that he had to stop swimming and when he did he was swept even more rapidly to the brink of the falls.

It was only necessary for him to free one arm because the power of the river soon dragged the jacket away from his body. Free at last of the encumbrance, he kicked for shore but the distance to the drop was less than twenty yards. He pulled with his arms and kicked with his legs as powerfully as he was able but he had only seconds before following the body of his assailant over the precipice.

The narrowing of the river, which Wes had noted when surveying ahead for a new beaching point, continued all the way to the lip of the waterfall. It meant that the more placid strip of water that had been a feature of the river's edge further upstream no longer existed, but reaching those large boulders which jutted into the river was now his only hope of survival. It was towards those that Wes directed his effort. If he failed to reach them or hold on to them he would certainly be swept to his death. The roar of the cascade filled his head as he made his effort. It was difficult to breathe without getting a mouthful of water but Wes swam on with grim determination.

The rocks were large and smooth due to the constant rush of water against them and he couldn't find anything to grip when he bumped against them. He was washed onwards, reaching out to find a handhold, the sinews of his arms stretched and aching with the futile efforts to arrest his forward propulsion. In a moment he would be swept to his doom. The last outcrop was before him and here he saw his last opportunity.

Along the edge of the cascade, like a set of bear's teeth, arose a handful of rocks. The river water crashed against them, throwing white spume many feet into the air. The gap between the rocks varied, but the two nearest the bank were less than a yard apart. Wes aimed for them, spreading himself to form a human dam. His arms grasped one and his thighs thumped against the other and, despite the force of water at his back, his body was stationary for the first time since he'd been dragged from the canoe. For several moments he hung between the two rocks, then scrambled atop one of them. From there he was able to find his way ashore.

2

From his stony perch, Wes watched the scrambling descent of the three men on the lower reaches of the far bank. Their route was a succession of drops, like a staircase of huge, steep steps. The leader of the trio lost his footing and tumbled head over heels for the last few yards. If his clumsiness attracted any sort of response from his companions it didn't carry above the crashing noise of the cascade. They were too far from Wes for their faces to be distinguishable, but one of them was wearing a short black jacket and a black hat and seemed to be issuing orders. The third man's attention was held by something across the river but the man in black dismissed any interest with a wave of his arm and turned away. Wes's view of the nearside bank was obscured by a rock formation and vegetation, so the object of the man's concern was unknown to him. In any case, the man who had fallen on his way down the escarpment had now retrieved three horses that had been tethered among the shrubbery and the men were soon mounted and racing downstream.

Beyond the foot of the waterfall the river widened, resulting in a less venomous flow. Some distance downstream Wes could see two other riders. They were stationed midstream, the water reaching to the top of their beasts' legs, their task clearly to collect anything worthwhile that floated towards them. By the time the other riders had come abreast of their position they had roped a bundle and were towing it to the bank for closer inspection. Wes had no doubt that it was his pack of pelts.

A desire for revenge for the attack on his life and the theft of his possessions settled in Wes's mind as naturally as singing hymns did for frontier folk at Sunday meetings. That was his way. No one took what belonged to him or threatened him with violence without repayment in kind. But underlying that need lay the thought that the ambush had been well planned, that it hadn't been a spur of the moment crime prepared for robbing him alone. The rope in the water, the obstruction at the landing place and the scavengers down river were all indications that this method of piracy had been well used. Wes wondered why. Travellers on the river were unlikely to be richly laden. In his own case, the money he would get for the pelts he'd brought with him was barely worth the trouble of setting traps. Even though there were traders and furriers who still bought good-quality hides and pelts it had been almost three decades since the end of the boom in the beaver trade. The worth of the pack that had been stolen was scarcely enough to cover the cost of his stopover in Council Bluffs. Even so, if he came across those men he would make them pay for its loss. Perhaps first, he'd ask why they'd done it, but that would only be to satisfy his curiosity. It wouldn't alter the outcome.

For now, thoughts of revenge had to be pushed to the back of his mind. Even as he watched, the men were spurring their horses in among the trees and were gone from sight. Currently, he had no means of catching or identifying them and the only weapon he had was the knife at his side. His new Winchester repeating rifle was somewhere at the bottom of the Missouri, probably at the foot of the falls, depending upon when it had parted company with the canoe. His sidearm, too, had gone into the river. Gun and belt had been wrapped among his change of clothing, deemed unnecessary and an encumbrance while paddling. He wouldn't have worn it again until he reached the *civilized* stretch of the river, where the American townships and settlements began.

Wes Gray wasn't the kind of man to

dwell on adversity. He had a need to reach Council Bluffs and many miles to cover in the accomplishment. Caleb Dodge would already be canvassing those planning to trek west; would have posted bills around town advertising his credentials as a wagon master and would by now, perhaps, have already held a meeting to inform people what he demanded of them if they chose to travel with him and, more important, what they needed to demand of themselves. Wes had heard the speech several times and didn't need to hear it again.

By the time he'd climbed down to the foot of the waterfall the high sun had dried his river-soaked clothing. Two objects were swaying in the water close to the foot of the falls. These, Wes assumed, were the cause of the agitation shown by the third man. One was the body of the man Wes had killed. The fall had broken so many bones that the movement of the limbs in the water was eerily unnatural. Whether his former friends knew the true cause of his death was uncertain, but as no one had taken the trouble to examine the corpse it seemed unlikely. Abandoning the body of a comrade was, in Wes's opinion, a callous act and indicative of the ruthlessness of the men who had attacked him. However, their neglect proved a point to his advantage because the second item in the water was his buckskin jacket. It had snagged on a rock and now, pulled by the current, billowed in such fashion that it appeared at first glance as though its wearer was face down in the water. A closer inspection would have revealed the truth of the matter, but the outlaws had been more concerned with capturing his goods. Wes was left to surmise that the outlaws believed that he, too, had been swept over the waterfall to his death.

Wes dragged the body ashore. It wasn't an act of respect for the dead man, simply an aversion to leaving him to rot and pollute the water. He dumped his would-be slayer on the bank. Wolves or wildcats would feast on him before the world was another day older. He retrieved his jacket, drained the water from it and resumed his journey.

He hadn't covered a hundred yards before a movement among the trees brought him to a standstill. The possibility that there were other members of the gang still in the vicinity hadn't occurred to him. The five he had seen ride away had done so as though satisfied that their work for that day was completed. He waited a moment but neither a challenge nor a bullet came his way. When the movement was repeated it was accompanied by a noise that Wes instantly recognized. Among the trees was the horse of the man he'd killed. It too had been abandoned; now it relieved Wes of the necessity of walking all the way to Council Bluffs.

Unbranded, the horse was able to offer no clue as to the identity of its owner. The saddle was old, suggesting perhaps that either the outlaw gang wasn't successful or the man had spent his money unwisely. There was a rifle in the saddle boot, a Springfield carbine, which in performance fell a long way short of the Winchester he'd recently acquired, but it was in working order and there was ammunition for it in the saddle-bags. Mounted and armed, Wes could now consider the possibility of tracking his ambushers.

He wasn't much more than an hour behind the bunch when he crossed the river at the point where his pack had been hauled ashore. He found the fresh tracks that led up among the trees to the higher ground beyond. The outlaws weren't making any attempt to cover their trail because they had no reason to suspect that they were being followed, a situation which was to Wes Gray's advantage. He was able to follow at an easy pace, thereby eliminating any risk of advertising his pursuit. They wouldn't ride all day and he would catch them when they made a halt.

Wes had been riding for more than an hour, climbing mainly, so that he doubted if he was yet four miles from the Missouri as the crow flies. He hadn't seen anything of the gang he was following and there were several stretches across bare rock where hoofprints didn't show, but he had no doubt that he was still in their wake. He had almost reached the crest of another ridge when from beyond he heard the unmistakeable crackling, rumbling sound of a rock slide. He pushed on up to the summit and dismounted. Looking down into the valley beyond it was easy to espy the location of the landslide. Off to his left arose a great grey cloud of dust which blotted from view the lower hillside pines.

For a few moments Wes scanned the slopes below him. Apart from the swirling dust there was no movement. Then, unexpectedly, a rifle shot cracked the air, giving Wes a point on which to focus. Immediately he saw them, three men whose shapes were becoming clearer through the dissipating dust. Currently, he was separated from them by about 400 yards, but to reach them, following the hillside trail, the distance would be at least twice as great. Two of the men had dismounted and as he watched, one of those fired a second shot into the dust that was still rising from further down the hillside. After a moment the men remounted and rode on.

Although the group consisted of only three riders, Wes had no reason to doubt that they were the men he was trailing, a conclusion endorsed by the dark apparel of one of those who had remained mounted. For a moment he considered leaving the trail, taking a direct line down the hillside, thereby shortening the distance between himself and those he sought, but he quickly set that thought aside. The dust that still hung above the lower stretches of the hillside was evidence enough that the scree-covered, steep descent was unstable. Even if another landslide didn't put him in physical jeopardy the kicked-up dust would surely advertise his presence to those below. Also, he had no knowledge of the capabilities of the horse beneath him. Wes couldn't predict how it would react to shifting stones beneath its hoofs.

Twenty minutes later he dismounted at the spot where his quarry had previously been. One of the men had discharged his rifle here but despite scanning the area Wes could find no obvious explanation for the shooting. Downhill, the course of the avalanche was clear to see. A narrow path had been formed by its passage: shrubbery uprooted or flattened and the rock face scarred where boulders had crashed against and skidded over the ground. Wes's instinct told him that there was something unnatural about the narrowness of the landslide's route. When he turned his attention to the uphill side of the trail his suspicions proved well-founded. The rockfall had been a man-made trap. There was evidence that a cradle had been constructed, in which the rocks and boulders had been stored. Logs, ropes and pulleys were scattered around, apparently tossed aside when the critical log, the linchpin, had been removed. Wes wondered why and by whom such a lethal trap had been set.

He also wondered about the rifle shots. What had been the gunman's target? He turned his attention once more to the more verdant downhill side of the trail but he couldn't see anything that provided an answer. He gathered the reins of the horse and was about to climb into the saddle when a noise, a sigh or a stifled groan, caught his attention. Whatever the noise was, Wes was certain that it was of human origin.

Once more he gave his attention to the land downhill from the trail. A breeze disturbed the grass and gently stirred the leaves of the nearby shrubs. He thought he heard the sound again; this time it was thinner, as though being carefully contained. Then there was a movement in a bush, too excessive to be caused by the breeze. When Wes fixed his gaze upon it its stillness seemed unnatural. Someone was watching Wes, anxious not to be discovered. When Wes heard the unmistakeable sound of the cocking of a revolver, he moved.

In a silent, crouching run he reached the shelter of some low boulders from where he could assess the situation. He had no pistol so once again resorted to using the long Bowie knife which had been his saviour earlier in the day. Concentrating on the bush from where the threat to his life emanated, he moved quickly, circling from the haven of the boulders to a point downhill from where he could see his would-be assassin. He had to assume that the man he could see was the fifth member of the group he was pursuing, although how they knew he was on their trail was a mystery to him. Perhaps one of them had lagged behind to watch their back trail, but Wes had been constantly alert, always scanning the ridges and horizon for just such a lookout. He was certain that he had not been under observation at any time, but the fact that a man now lay in wait for him seemed to prove otherwise.

The man behind the bush was hatless and wore grimy jeans with a bib and a red-checked shirt. Judging by his grey, thinning hair he was older than most of those who chose an outlaw's existence. There was something peculiar about the man's posture; his legs were indicative of a man in a supine position but the top half of his body was turned as fully as possible so that he could watch the trail above. It looked uncomfortable, but despite that Wes could see that his gun arm was steady. He would be a dangerous opponent.

Wes covered the ten yards between them so swiftly and silently that the man could not have been more surprised by an attack from an eagle swooping on him from above. The knife was at his throat and the pistol wrested from his grip in an instant. However, it was the automatic response of his body to the force of Wes's knee in his back that extracted from him a strangled yell of pain, and when he turned his head Wes could see that the man gripped a short stick between his teeth, a crude device to arrest any cries of pain. He spat it away and spoke through gritted teeth.

'Get it over with,' he snarled, 'because I ain't gonna tell you where it is. Just do it now, blast you.'

By this time Wes was sitting astride the old man's chest with the point of his Bowie knife at the other's throat. He examined the old man's weathered face, which was unnaturally pale.

'Joby?' he asked in surprise. 'Joby Patton?'

The old man barely heard his name spoken, he was too intent upon pouring scorn on any ploy that might be used to make him talk.

'It's all right, Joby. It's me, Wes Gray.' Wes stood up and regarded the man who was twisting in agony on the ground. The cause of his pain was immediately obvious. His right leg was broken and every movement was a source of torment.

3

When it came to the treatment of wounds and ailments Wes Gray's knowledge was restricted to the preparation of a few brews for breaking a fever and a compound for drawing snake venom from a bite: simple medicines he'd picked up while living with the Arapaho and travelling with other mountain men. He'd never had cause to treat himself with any of the remedies and, apart from once digging an arrowhead out of a partner's shoulder, had never practised doctoring on anyone else either. So his medical credentials weren't great and when he slit Joby's trousers to the knee and saw the severity of the fracture, his diagnosis was that the leg needed to be attended to by a professional physician.

That opinion brought a stubborn response from the old-timer. Ignoring the pain, Joby declared, 'You ain't taking me to Council Bluffs,' and he remained adamant on that point despite Wes's protestations. 'They think I'm dead,' he added, 'so they'll think they can come searching for my cabin and looting it whenever they choose. Well, they ain't getting it.'

The old prospector didn't elaborate on the 'it' but he spoke with such grim determination that it was clear to Wes that he was not going to win the argument. Joby associated any trip to Council Bluffs with the abandonment of his cabin, and anyone who proposed such a journey as part of a plot to pillage it.

'You need a proper doctor,' said Wes.

'No. You fix the leg.' Joby's eyes glared with a feverish intensity when he spoke. 'It's easy. Align the bone then fix it in place with tight-bound splints. I've done the same for other people.'

Wes was dubious but the prospect of transporting Joby down the hillside was no less daunting. A journey to Council

Bluffs wouldn't be easy. 'Let me get you to your cabin,' he said. 'I'll send the doctor up here.'

'I ain't taking you to my cabin and I don't want you showing anyone else where it is either. Just fix my leg here.'

Joby's attitude prompted a flash of anger. 'I'm not aiming to rob you,' Wes snapped, 'but even if I do some doctoring of your leg I can't leave you on the hillside afterwards.'

'I'll manage,' Joby grumbled, but it was evident that the wagon scout's words had made some impression.

'Suppose you tell me how this happened while I find some sticks for a splint.'

Before the onset of winter, Joby had panned the waters of a high creek and the assay office at Council Bluffs had assessed the dust samples as high-quality gold. He hadn't been back to Council Bluffs since the discovery, but word of the strike had spread and by spring several other men were working the various watercourses that led down from the high country. Unlike Joby, they announced their success in saloons and gambling dens, and among those who listened to their boasts were those who wanted to get their hands on the gold without bending their backs to pan it from the stream.

In the past few weeks more than one prospector with a poke full of gold dust had failed to reach Council Bluffs alive, ambushed on the hillside or on the river, all routes apparently being covered by the outlaw band. Wes figured it accounted for the attack on his canoe, that every traveller was assumed to be a successful gold-hunter and was therefore ambushed for his possessions. Although Joby hadn't yet made an attempt to reach Council Bluffs with the wealth he'd panned from the creek, the outlaws knew of his presence in the hills and had made previous attempts to capture him to reveal the location of his cache.

Until this day he had always outwitted them, had been aware of their approach and found a hiding-place until they'd gone. But this time they'd come across him before he'd had the opportunity to escape so he had lured them to this part of the mountain where he'd set this trap, one of several sites where he'd hidden weapons or set noose traps or boulder slides. Age, however, had affected his stamina and although he'd outrun his pursuers he'd been leaden-legged when he'd sprung the trap. Although the rock slide caught the robbers unawares and swept one of them to their death, he, too, had been struck by a boulder and bowled off the trail.

Because they'd seen his pack and hat carried away with their *compadre*, Joby believed that the outlaws had attributed him with the same fate. They'd fired shots at the falling rocks in frustration because they wanted him alive to tell them where his gold was hidden. He'd mistaken Wes for one of the gang, hanging around in case he'd survived the fall.

With nothing to deaden the pain and no one to hold the old man down, the task of setting the leg bone would have been a challenge for any man. Wes did all he could do, though he had no way of knowing how successful his effort was likely to be. Afterwards the old man slept, or perhaps he'd passed out, and Wes ruminated on the position in which he found himself. He had little hope now of catching those who'd stolen his pelts. The closer they got to Council Bluffs the harder it would be to identify one set of tracks from another on the well-used trail.

The thought that they might escape his wrath troubled him. Caleb Dodge, however, wouldn't yet be concerned by his non-appearance in Council Bluffs. The wagon master didn't need the services of his chief scout until the wagons were under way, but even so, his arrival couldn't be delayed indefinitely. His first concern, though, was Joby Patton, and despite the prospector's abrasive attitude Wes knew that he couldn't leave him alone on the hillside.

When Joby awoke, however, it was with an altogether different attitude. 'Wes Gray,' he said, as though surprised to see the scout at his side. A few minutes later, when he spoke again, it was to suggest the very course of action he'd opposed earlier. 'Get me to my cabin, Wes. There's something I need you to do for me.'

It took a deal of pain and cursing to get Joby on to the horse that Wes had claimed down by the river, but there was no alternative method of moving him across the hillside. It wasn't surprising that no one had found Joby's cabin, for it was deep in a concealed, crescent-shaped fold of the hills. Even if anyone chanced that way, any cursory inspection would find nothing but a dry-bed gorge. Wes helped the prospector inside and left him on his bunk while he prepared bacon, beans and coffee. Since his unexpected swim the previous day, Wes had eaten nothing but a handful of berries.

While they ate, Joby outlined the favour he required of Wes. 'My daughter, Anne, should now be in Council Bluffs. Bring her here,' he pleaded, 'secretly. I've found a rich vein,' he confided, 'but it needs to be worked by more than one man with a pick. I mean to sell my claim to one of the big mining companies. I'm ready to leave and I know a way out of these hills that will avoid going back to Council Bluffs. Anne and I will take it. We'll be gone from this territory before those outlaws find out that I'm still alive.'

Wes shook his head. 'I've got obligations. People heading west need me.'

'Pah!' Wes wasn't sure whether Joby's exclamation poured scorn on the idea of people walking halfway across the continent in search of a new life, or his own belief that his part in their trek was essential. His follow-up words proved that neither was the case. 'I'll pay you well. I've got gold, son. You fetch my daughter and I'll fill your pouch. Enough to cover your wagon-train pay for the rest of your life.'

'I don't want your gold, Joby. I told you that earlier. I promised to meet Caleb Dodge at Council Bluffs and that is what I'll do.'

'Reckon you've got time to get Anne up here and still meet up with those wagons. Won't take but a couple of days.'

'Couple of days to Council Bluffs and a couple of days back, but who knows how long it'll take to find her? Especially if I can't announce the fact that I'm looking for her.'

'She won't be difficult to find. Likely she'll be staying at the Pioneer House or the Western Star. Besides, you can't leave me here alone for too long. I'm running short of supplies and no way to get more unless you bring them.'

'The best answer is for me to take you down to Council Bluffs.'

'I'd be a dead man the moment I hit town. I saw those outlaws. I can identify them. You think they'll let me do that? No, Wes, I can protect myself here for a few days and it'll give my leg a chance to knit. You bring my daughter and a couple of pack animals back here and I'll be truly grateful.'

Wes Gray could find no more arguments. Caleb Dodge might puff out his cheeks at the thought of the wagons heading west without a chief scout but the reality of the situation was that Wes wasn't needed until they reached the first major river crossing. The wagons didn't reach the Blue River until they were almost two weeks out of Council Bluffs. Wes would be with them long before that.

* * *

With Wes Gray's agreement to his plan secured, the querulous and obstinate Joby Patton turned into a hard-headed, confident campaigner who knew exactly what he needed to do to protect himself and his home in the event of discovery.

Wes collected two rifles that had been concealed among rocks to add to the prospector's firepower, but left in place a Cheyenne lance which had been stuck upright into the ground behind a tree and an axe whose head was buried in a stump at the side of the cabin. In Wes's opinion, if attackers got into the cabin they would never give Joby the opportunity to use such weapons.

At daybreak Wes departed for Council Bluffs. It wasn't until late afternoon that he crossed trails with three men in a buckboard. He'd heard the rattle of their approach long before he saw them and reined in to the side of the trail until they passed. Their rough clothes suggested they were miners. The driver, a clay pipe gripped in his mouth, eyed Wes with uncertainty as they drew close. The other two held their rifles at the ready watching for any untoward move.

Wes held his hands above the horse's neck so that the miners could see he posed no threat. He recognized two of them, had played poker with them in the Drover's Bar the previous year.

'Howdy,' he said as they passed, but it wasn't until they were a few yards beyond that he heard one of the passengers say, 'It's OK. That's Wes Gray,' and belatedly a hand was raised in greeting.

'Gold,' thought Wes. 'It cripples a man's soul.'

The following morning, an hour beyond sunup, found Wes on the heavily wooded slope of a camel-humped hill which overlooked the Missouri. Running parallel with the river to a distant bend was the trail to Council Buffs. For several moments noises had carried to him from ahead and he had reined to a halt, scanning the trees for a sign of movement. He suspected that voices were mingled among the metallic rattles he could hear but, irrespective of whether they were or not, the noises were undoubt-edly man-made.

It took a minute to locate the source

of the commotion: three riders, each with a laden mule in tow, manoeuvring across the lower reaches of the descent. There was no mistaking the fact that they were prospectors or that they had recently abandoned the site they'd been working. Picks, shovels and sifting pans were lashed to the canvas-covered packs carried by the pack animals. The men themselves were travelling cautiously, casting glances all around as they made their way downhill to the well-worn trail below.

Wes Gray figured that they were determined not to suffer the fate that had befallen many of those gold-seekers who had traversed these hills before them. It was impossible to tell if they were partners or simply three men who had chosen to travel to Council Bluffs together in the hope that their being together would be sufficient to deter an attack from the outlaws.

It wasn't. Even as Wes watched their progress a sudden movement further down the hillside caught his attention.

A skittish, riderless horse disturbed the foliage of the bush to which it was tethered, and in so doing revealed another two riderless animals alongside. Instantly alert, Wes strained to catch sight of their owners. The fact that the horses were saddled reduced the possibility that the men were camped for an innocent breakfast. Instinctively, he pulled the Springfield from its scabbard.

At that moment a hand reached out for the reins of the excited horse, then the whole arm appeared as the hand moved to its muzzle, calming the beast, stilling it so that it didn't disturb the other two. Then the man came into total view, although presenting only his back to Wes. He was a squat man, wearing a red shirt and a white hat. The hand that wasn't consoling the beast held a rifle. Within seconds of his appearance he'd slipped once more from sight among the cluster of trees.

The prospectors were now only a hundred yards from the hidden horses and still cast glances all around as they journeyed onward. The antics of the misbehaving horse had not carried to them, had not heightened their caution.

Wes knew that the gold-hunters were riding into an ambush. Somewhere among the trees three men waited to rob them and, if Joby's account of events was accurate, kill them, too. He couldn't see the ambushers but the prospectors were getting ever closer. A shot in the air would provide some kind of warning, but until he spotted their location he could do little else.

The thought was no sooner in his mind than the first shot was fired from among the trees. Too late to give a warning, Wes fixed his sights on the place from where the small puff of smoke was rising and pulled the trigger. Suddenly, gunfire rang out in a flurry of shots, prospectors, ambushers and Wes all firing rapidly. Being caught in a crossfire startled the ambushers, not simply because the volley from above had been unexpected but because it was more accurate than the fusillade from the prospectors. After their initial volley at the threesome descending the hill, the ambushers turned their full attention on Wes, but bullets were singing close to where they crouched and splinters were flying from tree trunks and branches.

The cessation of lead flying in their direction gave the prospectors the chance to give greater accuracy to their own gunfire. Bullets peppered the foliage that the ambushers were using for cover and, realizing the danger of their situation, they were forced to make a dash for their horses. Two of them fired up hill to subdue the onslaught from Wes while the third, the man in the white hat, clambered into his saddle. Then he fired two shots towards the prospectors to give cover to his partners while they, too, mounted. In the brief abeyance of bullets being fired in his direction, Wes took careful aim and fired. He hit the first man mounted, the bullet striking his arm and causing him to drop his rifle as he twisted in the saddle, but all three put spur to horse and raced away between the trees.

Soon they were lost from sight. When they re-emerged they were at full gallop along the trail towards Council Bluffs. When Wes was sure that a renewed attack from them was not imminent he rode down to join the prospectors. Two of them watched his approach with rifles in hand, though they seemed to have little desire to use them. The third prospector lay on his back, legs and arms splayed. Half of his head was missing.

One of the survivors looked at Wes with bewilderment. 'What will I tell his ma?' he asked.

4

The last light of day was throwing weak, long shadows when Wes and the miners eventually reached Council Bluffs, a busy town which at this time of year was swelled with a hundred temporary canvas homes on the southern pastures. People from every eastern state were gathering together with a single aim: to restart their life on the far side of the Rockies. These were people excited by their hopes yet daunted by the undertaking, proud of their ambition yet anxious about the outcome; pioneers whose spirits were charged with the promise of free and fertile land but tempered by the anticipation of unknown trials.

Even so, as that small group moved slowly towards the sheriff's office those westbound pilgrims who happened to be on Main Street were as curious as the Council Bluffs citizens to discover what had befallen the man whose stiffening body was tied over the saddle of his horse. Comments and questions were thrown at the riders.

'Who is it, Abe?'

'My boy. They killed my boy.'

'Who done it?'

'We wuz ambushed. They'd have killed us all if Wes here hadn't pitched in.'

'Did they git your gold?'

'No. We fought them off.'

Sheriff Tom Beddow, notified of the approaching riders by an alert busybody, was on the porch outside his office when the men drew rein. Abe told the story from the back of his horse, gave details of where and when the attack had taken place. When he was done he took his boy's body to the undertaker; his partner went with him. Wes Gray dismounted and went inside with Tom Beddow. They had known each other for several years so the lawman had no hesitation in believing

Wes's additional tale about the attack on his canoe.

'Don't suppose you recognized anyone?'

'No, but the leader wore a short black jacket, black trousers and a black hat.'

The sheriff raised his eyebrows. 'Could be a man called Johnny Stoltz. He rides into town from time to time with a bunch of ne'er-do-wells, but I'd need a positive identification before I could go about arresting him.'

'Is he in town now?'

Tom Beddow didn't have a definite answer to that question, so Wes took him outside to examine the horse and carbine he'd commandeered. There was nothing about them that provided a clue to the identity of their dead owner but Tom said he would point out Johnny Stoltz if he came to town before Wes left with the wagons.

'I'm also looking for Joby Patton's daughter,' Wes said, then recounted his encounter with the old prospector. 'I don't know what she looks like or when she arrived but Joby expects her to be waiting here. Her name is Anne.'

Tom Beddow rubbed his chin, unable to suggest any of the newcomers to Council Bluffs as the person Wes sought.

'Guess I'll be visiting all the hotels and guest houses in the morning. I promised to get her to her father before heading west with Major Dodge.'

Uttering the major's name prompted Wes to go in search of the wagon master. He found Caleb eating dinner in Dorman's, a long restaurant on Jefferson Street. He was accompanied by Gil Forbes, his right-hand man, and they were engaged in some light-hearted conversation with the young woman who'd served their meal. Her hair was a light-brown colour, not fair enough to be called blonde nor ginger enough to be red. She wore a plain grey dress with a white apron over it. Wes thought he detected a trace of a Tennessee accent, but irrespective of her origin it was a voice full of warmth, as, too, was the glint in her brown eyes. Gil Forbes seemed little pleased by the abrupt end to the conversation caused by Wes's sudden arrival, but when the scout saw how Gil's eyes followed the girl back to the kitchen he understood the reason for the sour welcome.

'We've had to eat here every night,' Caleb explained, winking at Wes as he spoke. 'Still, Gil's lost his heart to less pretty girls in the past.'

Gil Forbes was on the point of protesting but stopped himself in time. He knew that proclaiming innocence of any interest in the girl would merely lead to a succession of good-natured taunts. Instead, by pointing out that the girl wore a wedding ring, he hoped to nip in the bud any further conversation on that topic.

'So I can count on you being with us all the way to California?' said Caleb.

'Reckon so.'

After the girl returned with the dish of stew that Wes had ordered, the three exchanged news and Wes explained his quest on behalf of Joby Patton. He also explained his need for an advance on his fee because his first task in the morning was to rearm himself. Caleb huffed and gruffed as Wes knew he would but there was never any doubt that the money would be forthcoming.

* * *

Since before the war, when Wes first reached Council Bluffs in company with other mountain men, he had done business with Ezzie Temple. Ezzie was the owner of the oldest emporium in Council Bluffs, and apart from selling such items as dry goods, tinned goods, fresh foods and clothing in the front part of the store, he also offered the services of fur trader, boot repairer and gunsmith at the rear. Weston Gray was an early visitor next morning. Ezzie was surprised that he had come without any pelts. He listened with sympathy as Wes related the events that had led to the loss of his pack.

'Something should be done about those robbers,' Ezzie declared, meaning that they should be caught and punished but, like most honest citizens, had no idea how to go about it.

Wes produced the Springfield carbine and Ezzie took it to the back part of his premises where he kept his stock of guns and tools for their maintenance. He inspected the Springfield carefully, eventually declaring that it had never passed through his hands at any time and that he didn't know to whom it belonged. Wes wasn't too disappointed by the verdict: it had, after all, been a slim chance that Ezzie had ever been asked to repair it. However, he tendered it in part-trade for a new Winchester and Colt .45, figuring that those who had stolen his pelts were still slightly ahead on the deal.

Rearmed to his satisfaction, Wes prepared to take his leave of his old friend and begin the search for Anne Patton, but as he turned to go a pile of beaver pelts caught his eye.

'Where did you get these?' he asked, picking up one bearing a distinctive dark stripe.

Ezzie took it from him, smoothed the pile in the manner of a true salesman preparing to close on a sale. 'Nice pelt.'

'Where did you get it?' Wes repeated.

'Fellow brought it in a couple of days ago.'

'That one and a few more,' suggested Wes.

Ezzie nodded. 'Said he'd been trapping higher up the Missouri.'

'Yeah, but hoping to trap pouches of gold. Do you mind if I look through the pack he brought in?'

Wes went through the collection, the belief that these were the pelts that had been stolen from him growing stronger with each moment that passed and each fur he inspected.

'Yours?' Ezzie asked.

'Mine, but I'd never be able to prove it. Who brought them in?'

'Don't know his name. Seen him

around town from time to time.'

'Has he sold pelts to you in the past?'

'No, but I had no reason to believe he'd stolen them. Like I said, he told me he'd been trapping up-river.'

It was too much to expect that Ezzie's description of the supplier would include black clothing but the term *stocky* was included together with reddish-coloured shirt and a yellow neckerchief. It was something to work with and the knowledge that the outlaws had been to Council Bluffs boded well for his chances of catching up with them. He thanked Ezzie for the information and headed off about his business.

Wes had one more bit of business to conduct before beginning his tour of the town's rooming establishments. As with the carbine, it was possible that someone could provide some information about the horse he'd commandeered and, if not, its value, too, would be offset against what had been stolen from him. If there were those who thought that the gun and horse were rightly the property of the descendants of the dead man, there were none that would say it publicly. No one would ever accuse Wes Gray of being a horse-thief to his face.

Each year he bought two horses from Luke Brandon, who owned the livery stable in Council Bluffs. Luke was acquainted with Wes's requirements. The horses had to be young, fit, supple and strong, and in addition, they had to demonstrate a level of eagerness and stamina that would remove from Wes any doubt in their ability to fulfil what he demanded of them. In short, between them they had to carry Wes over 1,500 miles in six months. There were always three or four satisfactory animals from which Wes would make his selection. At the end of the journey he would sell one and ride the other to the Wind River country. When spring came again and he took his leave of the people with whom he'd wintered, he would give the horse to his wife's father, Three Shoshones, a gift to one man which would be acknowledged throughout the tribe as a symbol of his unity with the Arapaho.

Luke Brandon hadn't been around the previous night when Wes had unharnessed the horse and turned it out into the corral behind the large wooden stable, but he'd given instructions to the young ostler to feed and groom it in the morning. The horse wasn't in the corral when he arrived and voices drifted to Wes as he approached the open doors.

'Wes Gray brought him in last night,' the unmistakable voice of Luke Brandon declared.

'Wes Gray!' The second voice was gruff and, in its repetition of the name, held a note of trepidation, as though Luke had made a mistake, or there was another man by the name of Wes Gray whose reputation wasn't that of the frontiersman who was feared by red and white men alike. 'The squaw man?'

'Don't know any other,' said Luke

Brandon. There was a pause before he spoke again, this time his tone bearing a touch of impatience. 'So what do you want to do about it? I expect Wes will be here soon. You'll be able to make your enquiries direct if you hang around.'

'Enquiries about what?' Framed in the doorway with the new day's light behind him, Wes was an imposing silhouette.

'Howdy, Wes,' called Luke Brandon. 'Heard you were in town. This fellow thinks the horse you brought in belongs to a friend of his.'

'No,' said the man quickly. 'There's a resemblance. I guess I'm mistaken.' He began to walk towards the door, head lowered, intending to pass Wes without any more conversation.

Wes moved slightly, a little to his right, not blocking the man's route but transmitting the message that he could do so if it became necessary. The man looked up. He wasn't as tall as Wes but broad and tough-looking. Stocky was a good description and as he moved more into the light Wes could distinguish his dirty red shirt and a yellow neckerchief that was bordered with small black spots. Another step closer and it was apparent that the sideburns that reached almost to the man's chin bore enough redness in their colour for him to match the description of the man who had sold Wes's pelts to Ezzie Temple.

'Where's your friend now?' asked Wes.

The man's answer consisted of a few unrelated words, an attempt at bluster, trying to persuade Wes that he had no right to question him while at the same time wary that something he said would incur the mountain man's wrath.

'The man who owned that horse was part of a gang that robbed me,' Wes told him. Wes held the man's gaze, watched as a series of twitches and eye movements betrayed his nervousness at the confrontation. 'I killed him.' For a handful of seconds the words hung in the air. 'And you,' Wes continued, 'fit the description of the man who sold my stolen pack to Ezzie Temple.'

'That's a lie.'

'Suppose we ask Ezzie about that. See if he identifies you.'

'You've got no right to accuse me of stealing your pelts.'

'Who said the pack consisted of pelts?' The two men faced each other. Wes Gray's immobility was as that of an iceberg and the gaze he settled on the other man was just as cold. 'Only the robber would know that.'

The man in the red shirt licked his lips. The word that circulated about Wes Gray was that he knew a hundred Indian ways to kill a man, all of which, it was implied, involved unspeakable torment. He could still hear Wes's own voice, deliberate and chilling, echoing in his head. *I killed him*. Suddenly, as though spurs had been roughly applied to his backside, he moved. He grabbed a halter from its peg on the wall and flung it at Wes while making a dash to evade his taller adversary.

A buckle caught Wes high on the cheek and momentarily his hands were fully engaged with the tangle of leather straps that had been thrown at him. But he'd anticipated the other's attempted escape and thrust out a leg as he passed, tripping him and sending him crashing into the thick wooden planks of a stall. A horse snorted and stamped.

Rubbing his shoulder, the man in the red shirt got to his feet, then dropped his hand to his six-gun. Wes leapt across the space that divided them, his hands grasping at the wrist that held the pistol and his weight carrying the man once more against the wooden enclosure. The gun discharged, the shot resounding in the confines of the stable, the bullet striking and embedding into one of the walls.

Rolling together on the ground they grappled for possession of the gun. Wes still held on to the other's wrist with his left hand, keeping the weapon pointed away from himself but conscious of the fact that Luke Brandon could be the victim of a stray shot as indeed could any of the valuable beasts in the stable.

Wes tried to throw a punch with his right hand but without a lot of success. Lying atop his opponent meant it was impossible to generate a lot of power into the blow and this was reduced further by the man underneath attempting to knee him in the groin. Wes tried again and a similar outcome convinced him that a different strategy was necessary. His first priority was to disarm the man.

The man in the red shirt struggled furiously, bucking and twisting in an attempt to dislodge Wes, his efforts barely subsiding even when Wes pressed his right forearm against the other's throat, depriving him almost completely of air. But it did mean that the whole of his concentration became focused on his need to remove that obstacle. Consequently, the six-gun was prised from his grip and discarded he knew not where.

Regaining his feet, Wes dragged the man up, too. 'Who else?' he asked.

Coughing and spluttering the man made a great show of needing air before he could answer. He bent forward at the waist, hands on knees, panting, needing to take in great breaths. But the man wasn't as incapacitated as the performance indicated. As Wes released his hold on his shirt, the man lunged backwards with his right arm, plunging his elbow into Wes's midriff. As Wes staggered backwards the man ran to the far side of the alleyway in which they'd fought and reached for a pitchfork propped against the stable wall. With the tines pointed at Wes he advanced.

It would have been a simple matter for Wes to draw his new Colt and kill the man instantly. Such a course of action crossed his mind but was discarded immediately. This man could identify the other gang members and Wes intended that they would all pay for the attempt on his life. Reaching to his side he withdrew the Bowie knife, moved it from hand to hand, leaving his opponent in no doubt that he was well versed in its use. He crouched slightly and dipped his shoulders in the other's direction.

Sweat broke out on the red-shirted man's brow. The big knife in Wes Gray's hands reminded him of the words: *a hundred Indian ways to kill*. With a shout he jumped forward, stabbed the pitchfork at Wes Gray's stomach, only to find that the frontiersman had already moved. With catlike stealth, Wes had sidestepped and now he chopped down with his weapon's heavy blade, shattering the shaft of the pitchfork and unbalancing the man who held it. As Red-shirt stumbled, Wes stepped behind him and in an instant had the man at his mercy. Securing the other's neck in the crook of his left arm, Wes pressed the point of his knife against his throat.

'Names,' he growled. 'Who else was involved?'

At that moment a shot was fired and, from behind, the voice of Sheriff Tom Beddow demanded, 'Put the knife away, Wes, or I'll shoot to kill.'

5

Confronted by the law, the man in the red shirt gave his name as Chuck Bodine, then angrily repudiated Wes Gray's contention that he had been involved in piracy and attempted murder. He admitted selling pelts to Ezzie Temple but claimed they were the result of honest labour, taken from beaver he had trapped along a northern tributary of the Missouri. Without any proof in support of Wes's claim, Tom Beddow had no alternative but to send Bodine on his way and issue a warning to Wes that he wouldn't tolerate a feud developing between them.

'Bring me evidence that the furs belong to you and I'll arrest that man,' he declared, 'but until you do the law is on his side. Stay away from Bodine, Wes.'

Wes had no wish to cause trouble for

Tom Beddow and accepted the warning with a shrug of his shoulders, but he watched Bodine as he strode further along the street towards the Long Lariat saloon. Before pushing through the batwing doors, Bodine paused and looked back towards the livery stable. Despite the distance between them, they held each other's gaze; grim expressions which were ended when a nervous sneer curled the corners of Bodine's mouth before he disappeared into the whiskey palace. At present, Bodine had the best of the situation but both men knew that the matter was not yet settled.

It took the best part of an hour for Wes to select two animals from Luke Brandon's stock. Four horses took his eye but after checking them and riding each for a short stretch across the meadow north of town, he plumped for a chestnut mare and a roan gelding. The price he paid included the cost of stabling while he remained in Council Bluffs. Both men were satisfied with the deal.

With that task accomplished, Wes turned his attention to the search for Joby Patton's girl. When he'd mentioned her to Tom Beddow and Ezzie Temple they had been surprised to learn of her existence. Although the old miner had spent a lot of time around town he had never disclosed details of his earlier life. Consequently, neither man was able to provide information as to her current whereabouts. Sheriff Beddow was sure that no one of the name Anne Patton had arrived in town recently, but he posed the possibility that she was on one of the wagons waiting to head west.

That suggestion didn't sit easy with Wes. If he'd understood Joby correctly, the old man had sent for his daughter several weeks ago and believed her to be waiting for him here in Council Bluffs, so searching for her among the westbound travellers would be a last resort. Wes's first enquiries would be at the hotels and boarding houses of the town. This, of course, made a mockery of Joby's demand for caution. Perhaps, when he found her, Wes would be able to get Anne Patton out of town secretly, but first he had to find her and that couldn't be done without asking questions. Unfortunately, lobby clerks in hotels and ladies who ran boarding houses had always proved to be the biggest gossips in every place he'd been.

As Wes Gray made his way from one lodging place to another, from the best hotel to the most humble home with a room to let, it became clear to him that, apart from her name, he knew nothing about the girl he was seeking. He didn't know her age, her height or the colour of her hair, nor did he know if she had the financial means to support herself while awaiting her father but, irrespective of his lack of details, the answer he got at every establishment he visited was the same. No one had heard of Anne Patton.

It was the hottest part of the

afternoon and Wes was contemplating a cold beer when Tom Beddow hailed him from across the street.

'Had a talk with Clem McGann,' the sheriff began, nodding towards the assay office further down the street, 'asked if he'd done any recent business with strangers. Figured that the robbers wouldn't want to hang on to stolen gold any longer than necessary so they might have made a beeline for his place, to turn it into paper dollars. But it ain't happened. According to Clem, the only people he's seen have been the regular grubbers who come to town as soon as they have enough to satisfy their immediate needs of a steak meal, a wild whiskey celebration and a bed at one of the good-time houses behind Main Street.'

He paused a moment, looked around as though wanting to be sure there was no one close enough to hear what he said next. 'But he says there's a rumour around town that Joby Patton is dead. Doesn't know how it started or where he first heard it but it seems to be common gossip.'

Wes and Tom agreed that whoever had started that rumour had probably been involved in the attack on Joby Patton, so they headed in the direction of the small, mainly wood-built structure that was the assay office to requestion Clem McGann. It was possible that he'd remembered something that could be helpful since his earlier talk with the sheriff, or, perhaps together, they could loosen more details from him.

Clem McGann was behind a desk when Wes and Tom Beddow entered. He was jacketless, his white cotton shirt was spotless and a long black ribbon was tied in a bow under its collar. His shoulders were broad and when he stood to greet his visitors he reached a height that was three or four inches greater than Wes. Also, he was younger than Wes and when he spoke he oozed confidence.

'I can't tell you any more than I've

already told the sheriff,' he declared in answer to Wes's prompt for more details about the rumour. 'All I can say is that if it is true then whoever stumbles on his claim will be very lucky. The dust he brought in last year was of the highest quality.'

'It isn't true,' Tom Beddow told him, 'and even if it was the strike belongs to Joby's daughter.'

'Daughter! I wasn't aware he had any family.'

'We think she's here in Council Bluffs,' said Sheriff Beddow. 'Wes here is trying to find her to take her to her father's cabin. He's spent the day searching the hotels and rooming houses but hasn't found her yet.'

That was information that Wes would rather not have had disclosed. Clearly, Joby had kept the existence of his daughter a secret from the citizens of Council Bluffs and even though half the town was now aware that Wes was looking for a girl called Anne Patton no one had had cause to associate her with the irascible prospector.

Accepting that the government agent had nothing more to tell, Wes and the sheriff took their leave of Clem McGann.

On the street, two horsemen drew to a halt as they parted company. Caleb Dodge called to him. 'Gil and I are heading out to talk with some of the settlers on the south meadow. It would be a good time to introduce my chief scout to them.'

Wes shook his head. 'I'm still looking for Joby's daughter. Sooner I locate her the sooner I can give full attention to getting those people across the Rockies.'

'Mean to start next week,' stated Caleb. 'Need you with me, Wes.'

'I know,' he answered. 'If I'm not here when you leave I'll meet you at the Blue River to help with the crossing. You have my word on that.'

Caleb Dodge fixed Wes with a hard-eyed stare. There was no other man to whom he would give such leeway, but Wes had proved himself worthy of his trust. He gave a curt nod. 'We'll be having dinner at Dorman's eating place later. Join us.'

'Depends on what I turn up,' Wes replied and watched for a moment as the major and Gil Forbes rode away.

Wes never knew that one town could have so many places with rooms to let for weary travellers. By the end of the afternoon he was sure he had visited every one, being directed from one address to another by helpful citizens, but none proving fruitful in his hunt for Joby's daughter. When he returned to his room at the Missouri Star Hotel it was in the belief that Anne Patton had not arrived in Council Bluffs.

Needing to think out his next move, Wes chose to eat alone that night, taking a table in his hotel rather than seeking out Caleb and Gil at Dorman's diner. He had finished his meal, was drinking the last of the coffee in his cup when a man and woman approached his table. She was a slim girl with high-piled red hair upon which sat a black hat complete with veil and feather. She wore a long grey travelling coat and carried a small bag the same colour as her hat. Her voice, when she spoke to Wes, was smooth, and pleasant to hear. It projected a warm personality which suggested that the girl was both intelligent and confident.

'Mr Gray?' she asked, but the question was rhetorical because she continued without his need to answer. 'I understand you're looking for me. My name is Anne Morphy. I'm Joby Patton's daughter. This is my husband, Frank Morphy.'

Frank Morphy was probably twenty years older than his wife, a situation which was not uncommon among the settlements further west but which, in this instant, surprised Wes. Whereas Anne Morphy was neat, fresh and cultured, her husband was not. The most prominent feature of his face was a scar which ran from his left ear to his chin, a knife wound which Wes felt sure the man had been lucky to survive, and his skin was swarthy, as though it bore an uncleanliness that no amount of washing would ever change. His manner was more that of a trail-drive cowboy than that of a consort for such an eastern-bred beauty.

But relief at the arrival of the girl proved greater for Wes than consideration for the differences between this man and woman. She seemed well-enough pleased with her husband as she explained that they were recently married, were in fact on their honeymoon, the marriage having been brought forward to avert the need for her to travel alone in answer to her father's summons.

'And you are to take me to my father,' she said.

The girl's words were a statement not a question, carrying with them a sense of urgency which surprised Wes. Indeed the girl's impatience to be about the journey was greater than the frontiersman had supposed, for his proposal to make an early start in the morning was countered by her declaration that she could be ready to travel within the hour.

Frank Morphy agreed with her. 'We can cover a few miles before darkness,' he told Wes, a thin smile stretching across his face which, even if it and his statement were meant to show confidence in his new wife's capabilities, struck a sour note with Wes.

Even so, an immediate start held advantages for Wes. Not only was their departure likely to draw less attention at an hour when most people were in their homes or dining in one of the town's many eating places, but the sooner he was free from this obligation the earlier he would be able to join up with Caleb and the wagon train. Even so, because of Joby's need for two pack animals, Wes decided that they shouldn't leave town together. Three riders accompanied by two spare horses would be sure to arouse interest. It was agreed that Frank and Anne would ride out with one additional horse and Wes, with the other horse, would meet up with them a mile north of town.

Because he lived on the premises, Ezzie Temple's hours of business were flexible, usually extending until the night hours when only the palaces of pleasure were open. This night was no exception and it became Wes's first stop after quitting the hotel. He didn't need much in the way of provisions because his little party would be only two nights on the trail before reaching Joby Patton's shack, but he left an order for the trader to fill while he attended to business at the livery stable.

A bunch of men were gathered at the stable door when Wes approached Luke Brandon's place. Luke himself was out front scratching his head like he'd been set a conundrum which was well beyond his intellect to solve. Luke shook his head, a denial to a question that had been posed, and it took a moment for Wes to recognize the questioner as Sheriff Tom Beddow. The lawman waved an arm at Luke as he turned away, a gesture that signified acceptance of whatever contribution Luke had made to the discussion. Tom Beddow walked away with the rest of the group in his wake. Halfway across the street he stopped and spoke to his acolytes. When he was done they split into two groups, the first, led by himself, headed towards the buildings on the far side of the street while the remainder made their way towards a cross-street which led to the less opulent area of Council Bluffs.

Luke Brandon chuckled when Wes reached him. 'They've lost the song-and-dance man,' he said. 'Star attraction at Riordan's Palace has gone missing. Tom Beddow says that Mike Riordan is close to bursting a blood vessel. The man arrived in town this morning, borrowed Mike's rig this afternoon and hasn't been seen since. I don't know if Mike is more concerned for his missing horses or the fact that he hasn't got an artist when the curtain goes up tonight.'

Wes understood the reason for Luke's amusement. Stories of theatrical failures were widespread in frontier towns and Michael Riordan had had more than his share over the years, but to the best of Wes's knowledge this was the first time that one of his acts had run off with his horses and buggy.

'Tom has sent out riders in case the man has had an accident,' Luke continued. 'Meanwhile he and some good citizens are searching the likely establishments of the town where a man might want to clear away any trail dust from his throat. I reckon few of them will get home sober this night.' He chuckled again.

Anxious to be about his business, Wes saddled the gelding he'd bought and left the chestnut mare in her stall to be collected when he returned. He agreed a price for a staunch black gelding which he adjudged fit enough for Joby's purpose, then led the two horses out of the livery stable and down the street to

Ezzie's store, where he filled a linen bag with some provisions for the trip ahead.

'Tell Caleb I've found Joby's daughter,' Wes told the storekeeper, 'and that I'll catch up if he's gone before I return.' When he climbed into the saddle he felt the eagerness of the roan beneath him but kept it on a short rein while they travelled the length of the town's main street.

He was almost at the end of the street when Gil Forbes, Caleb Dodge's right-hand man, arrived at Ezzie Temple's emporium. He called after Wes but the frontiersman was at that moment passing the last saloon bar and the tinny sound of a heavily played piano was flooding into the street. Wes put his horse to a canter and hurried away out of sight as the street narrowed into the northern trail along the bank of the Missouri.

As they stood side by side, gazing along the now empty street, Ezzie passed on the messages to Gil. 'He's not deserting Caleb,' he said, 'but he's found Joby Patton's daughter and he's taking her to her father.'

Gil Forbes looked at Ezzie; his face wore a bemused expression.

6

They crossed the river at an oft-used ford where the water was little more than shin high on the animals. They were six miles north of Council Bluffs and at the outset, when they met on the outskirts of that town, Wes had explained to Anne and Frank Morphy that they wouldn't get more than ten miles that day, citing not only the limitation imposed by the oncoming darkness but also the fact that if seen riding hard with two lightly loaded packhorses it would mark them out for attention. Even so, it had been Wes Gray's aim to cross the Missouri at this point before nightfall because he knew of a suitable site where they could bed down: one that provided a commanding view of the river so that anyone on their trail would be easily spotted.

It wasn't until they dismounted that

Wes became aware of the girl's unkempt wardrobe. Her ill-fitting trousers were coarse denim and gathered at the waist with a broad leather belt. The rough cotton shirt she wore was clean but frayed and smeared with old axle-oil stains. Tied around her neck was a dull grey scarf. It hung in heavy folds upon her chest as though in waiting to cover her face, like she'd been asked to ride drag on a cattle-drive or was waiting to rob a stagecoach. Her hair was hidden from sight, tucked up inside an old grey slouch hat, which sat low on her head. It was hard to believe that this was the same girl in the elegant clothes who had approached him at the hotel. Then, she had looked very much like a young lady of refinement.

Frank Morphy, noticing Wes's interest in his wife's apparel, offered an explanation. 'Some of my old clothes,' he said. 'We didn't come prepared to travel beyond Council Bluffs and there was no time for shopping at the store.'

The words were glib and the smile which accompanied them supercilious, as though courting Wes's disbelief because he was certain of his own ability to deceive. Wes didn't argue, he was going to be in Frank Morphy's company for only another two days, but his explanation didn't match the statement he'd made at the hotel, that he and Anne were ready to leave within the hour.

Wes picketed the horses while the others laid out their bedrolls. Later, they gathered around a small fire and drank coffee but there was little conversation. Wes said that he would keep watch from a higher rock for signs of pursuit, an announcement greeted by Frank Morphy with the sort of grin he had displayed earlier.

'Shouldn't think anyone followed us from Council Bluffs,' he said.

'Her pa says there are men who'll stop at nothing to get his gold. I've been involved in incidents in this stretch of country that make me believe him. I promised to get his daughter to him and that means taking precautions. I'll watch for a couple of hours; if nothing moves I'll come back here. Meanwhile I suggest that you and your wife get some sleep. Tomorrow will be a long day in the saddle.'

Frank Morphy touched his hat, a gesture almost as contemptuous as his smile. 'Anything you say, Mr Gray.' He moved away to where his blankets and saddle were his bed.

Sitting on her own blankets, Anne Morphy watched from a position some twenty yards away from the small fire, her eyes following Frank's progress in the opposite direction, wary, it seemed to Wes, lest he should approach. But Frank didn't look in her direction, didn't even cast a word towards his wife. Strange behaviour, Wes thought, for newly married folk, but it was none of his business. All he had to do was get the girl to her father, then he could get back to Council Bluffs. The girl looked his way while he still studied her. For a moment their eyes met, then Anne Morphy looked down, deliberately avoiding his gaze, wary, he supposed, of his interpretation of the coldness between husband and wife. She lay down and covered herself with her blanket.

Wes squatted above the little camp as the light waned, perched with rifle across his knees until the sky became the deep blue of midnight against which the jagged, silhouette line of the surrounding trees was etched. It was at moments like this that he was most content; alone with the smell of the trees, the sound of a nearby river and now and then the sight of an animal making its way to the water. Occasionally the disturbance of an undergrowth struggle would reach him as predator and prey undertook the age-old battle for survival. But finally, satisfied that the stillness of the night was broken only by the nocturnal habits of the animals of the forest, he had to admit that Frank Morphy's assessment on the topic of pursuit was correct. No one had followed them from Council Bluffs. He propped his rifle against a high rock, pulled his hat over his eyes and slept.

Next day they were on the move shortly after sunrise. Wes led the way with one of the spare horses on a short rein at his side. Anne Morphy followed and her husband rode in the rear, trailing the other pack animal. Few words were spoken during the journey and most of those that were came from Wes: instructions as to the care of their animals whenever he called a rest. He might have expected questions from Anne Morphy to glean more information about his relationship with her father, but none were forthcoming and, as they travelled, each time he looked back to confirm that all was well with those behind, her gaze seemed to be fixed on the same spot between her horse's ears. In the light of day she seemed a lot less comfortable astride her dun mare than he had supposed she would be the night before. However, while she was devoid of conversation, she was also devoid of complaints; she made do with whatever pace Wes set and accepted whatever halts he called.

Although the lack of communication between himself and the Morphys was unexpected, Wes was even more surprised by the unsolicitous manner of Frank Morphy towards his wife. Not once did he hear any exchange of words, not even a whispered word of encouragement as the day wore on and the climb into the high ground became steeper. It wasn't an easy ride even though they had stuck to the recognized trail, such as it was. Despite the knowledge of bandits in the hills, Wes hadn't deviated from the road the miners had used for the past year, his decision made in consideration of the unproven horsemanship of Anne Morphy. He was still unsure of her capabilities but her determination wasn't lacking.

Because of the attacks on Joby Patton

and the other miners when heading towards Council Bluffs, Wes kept a sharp lookout for signs of an encounter with the gold robbers. He figured they were probably safe from attack as the usual prey was the people coming down from the hills, who were likely to be carrying dust and nuggets, but outlaws were outlaws and in the absence of a more lucrative target, liable to stop the threesome and take whatever wealth they had.

It was late afternoon when they stopped to rest and water the horses. Anne Morphy went a little way downhill, rubbing her face as she walked with the end of the scarf that hung around her neck. Her husband watched her, his gaze unwavering, but his face failed to register any pleasure.

Wes noted Frank Morphy's cold, hard stare. 'You shouldn't let her go too far alone,' he said. 'There may be outlaws in the area.'

Frank turned his attention to Wes. 'She'll be fine,' he assured the scout.

'Even so,' said Wes, 'we need to get started and I don't want to shout to bring her back. Noise carries on the hillside. We don't want to betray our presence, do we?'

With a shrug of his shoulders, an indication that he thought Wes's caution too extreme, Frank set off to catch up with his wife. While checking the harnesses of his riding-horse and the two pack animals, Wes's thoughts dwelt once more on the incongruity of Anne and Frank Morphy as man and wife. It wasn't merely the age difference that seemed off kilter, nor, indeed, the difference in their circumstances: Wes well knew that those things had less importance the further west the frontier was pushed. It was the distance the two people maintained between themselves. He had to admit that the lack of conversation meant that he didn't know anything about the Morphys, but it was that same lack of conversation that made him think they didn't know anything about each other.

With the last girth tightened he let his gaze wander downhill. Anne Morphy was returning, had passed her husband and was walking, as elegantly as her ill-fitting clothes would allow, back to where Wes waited. Frank, however, was motionless, his eyes fixed on the trees of their back trail. The distance between them was too great for Wes to be certain of the other's sight-line but nonetheless, he scanned the wooded slopes. If something had caught Frank's attention he hoped he would see it, too. Moving his head slowly he made a barren search from left to right. The return sweep was executed even more slowly but seemed likely to produce the same result until the hint of a movement caused him to refocus on a point to his right. Had there been a figure among the trees or had it been the shadow of a drifting cloud? Perhaps it had been nothing more than the movement of foliage disturbed by the breeze. Whatever, it didn't recur and Frank Morphy was now following his wife up the trail.

'Man should pause awhile and enjoy God's creation,' Frank told Wes when the frontiersman asked what had caught his attention.

'You didn't see anyone? Anyone who might be following us?'

Frank spread his arms. 'Who would be following us?' His answer was meant to convey confidence in their journey and banish completely any suggestion that claim-jumpers were after his father-in-law's mine, but he couldn't prevent the grin touching his face. Even though he turned away as it began, the sly and supercilious expression didn't escape Wes. He didn't like Frank Morphy, didn't trust him. He looked towards his wife to take note of her reaction, but Anne was already mounted, eyes fixed, once more, on the back of her horse's head.

They travelled until dusk, Wes's senses working even harder to detect any indication of either pursuit behind or ambush ahead. Surreptitiously he watched the behaviour of Joby Patton's daughter and her husband but their behaviour didn't alter; neither spoke until Wes picked out a spot as their campsite for that night.

'Another early start and we'll reach your pa's cabin mid-morning,' Wes told Anne when she asked how much further they had to travel. It was information she didn't pass on to Frank but he had been unsaddling his horse and had, Wes suspected, overheard.

It was while Wes was gathering dry sticks to build a small fire that he caught the smell of smoke. It was faint, drifting, intermittent, dissipated by the light evening breeze, but its source was clearly on their back trail. While he and his companions had not been travelling as though they were in a race against time, nor had they dallied, and as the fire that he could smell was probably less than a mile away it was clear that the pursuers could only have got so close by hard riding.

Neither Anne nor Frank picked up

the scent of smoke and neither of them commented when the disturbed horses snorted their concern. Wes chose to keep the information to himself, waited until they'd fed on oatcakes and coffee and retired to their bedrolls, which, in the absence of conversation, didn't take long. It had been a long day and Anne had looked weary from the moment they'd dismounted. Turning her back to the small, dwindling fire she was soon asleep. Frank shuffled and coughed a while longer but eventually he, too, became silent and when Wes was satisfied that both of his companions were asleep, he, too, closed his eyes.

Wes woke an hour before dawn, listened for movement from the others and when content that neither was awake, grabbed his rifle and stepped stealthily away from the camp. Avoiding the worn trail, feet encased in his customary soft moccasins, he moved swiftly and silently, shadow-like, across the uneven landscape. A little light was cast by a moon on the wane but it was sufficient for a man who had raided Crow villages with Sioux war parties. Ten minutes later he had found his quarry, the smoke from their smouldering fire drawing him like a magnet to the bare rock enclosure in which they'd settled.

Wes worked his way around the small camp, pausing after each careful step, watching for movement either near the fire or among the boulders beyond. He counted two people wrapped in blankets, one either side of the remaining ashes, but that didn't mean that there weren't others on guard, guns primed as a precaution against invaders. On he moved, completing a half-loop that brought him to the far side of the camp. Here he discovered two horses tethered to low bushes. The number was significant, confirming that pursuit was confined to the two around the fire.

Dawn was approaching, night's blackness easing to a diabolical grey and shapes were forming as though seen through thick smoke when Wes approached the sleepers. He lifted a rifle from one saddle boot and a handgun from a nearby holster. He couldn't find the weapons of the second person; figured they were concealed under the covering blanket, so he sat awhile, waiting until the light was stronger, thus ensuring that no threatening movement went unnoticed. Then he kicked at the soles of their feet and covered them with his rifle as they jumped awake.

'Don't do anything quickly,' he told them. 'Just crawl away from your blankets. Come over here, towards me and spread out your arms and legs.'

Before he'd finished speaking the one who had been armed sat upright, startled, his head turning to the sound of the voice, but when he spoke his own voice registered surprise, as though he might still be in a dream.

'Wes? Wes Gray, is that you? It's me. Gil Forbes.'

'Gil? What are you doing here?'

'Trying to catch you,' Gil grumbled.

Wes uncocked his rifle and squatted beside Caleb Dodge's assistant. He was puzzled by Gil's pursuit, he couldn't believe that he had been sent by Caleb. The major, he was certain, had faith enough to know that he would be at the Blue River when needed.

'I tried to catch you before you left Council Bluffs,' Gil said, 'but I was just too late.'

'What is so important? Couldn't it wait until I got back? I thought you were part of the gang who have been robbing the miners.'

'Well, we aren't,' said Gil, ignoring the first two questions, 'and we're here because there's something you need to know.' He looked across the ashes of the fire to the other figure awakened by a kick from Wes. 'You were scouring Council Bluffs for Joby Patton's daughter. Well, there she is.'

Wes too turned his attention to the other person. For the first time he realized it was a woman. Closer examination of her face proved her to be the person who had served them at Dorman's restaurant, the one who had sparked Gil Forbes.

'Joby's daughter is further along the trail,' Wes said, 'with her husband.'

The woman answered. 'I don't know who those people are, Mr Gray, but they are impostors. I was married, but my husband was killed during the war. I'm Mrs Anne Cowell but I daresay my father forgot to inform you of that. His letters are still addressed to Anne Patton.'

Wes Gray didn't know what to believe. He cast looks at Gil Forbes and the woman in turn. Both wore earnest expressions but Wes knew he would discount any testimony from Gil because he was happy to repeat anything this woman told him.

'I lived in Des Moines for several years,' the woman said. 'Last winter my father paid a surprise visit, bringing news of a rich gold strike. He urged me to move closer to his claim because he suspected that claim-jumpers and robbers might force him to quit the area in a hurry. We settled on Council Bluffs because it would be easier to pass undetected amongst all the spring arrivals who would be gathering to head west. I decided I'd be less noticeable if I took a job and the restaurant provided a room, too. When Gil told me you were searching for Anne Patton on behalf of her father I owned up to the fact that I was the one you were seeking.'

Gil spoke again. 'By the time I'd traced you to Ezzie Temple's store you were leaving town. When Ezzie passed on your message we figured you'd been duped by the robbers and were leading them to Joby's mine. We set out at daybreak to catch you.'

Wes Gray studied the woman's face; he could see nothing in it that brought Joby Patton to mind, but the same could be said of the girl he'd left sleeping further ahead. A name was the only means of identification he had been given and now both claimants had confused matters by virtue of marriage.

His search for Anne Patton had become general knowledge in Council Buffs but linking her to the lonely prospector was not a natural progression. Few people in that town had any knowledge of Joby's history yet both of these girls professed to be his daughter. His dilemma was etched on his face.

'I have something that will convince you that I'm telling the truth,' said the woman. She began a search through a canvas travelling bag.

The proof was a certificate setting out the location of Joby's claim from the Des Moines land registry office. 'He left the deeds with me for safe-keeping,' she told Wes, 'and so that I could prove the gold was mine if anything happened to him.'

As he read the document the girl spoke again. What she said convinced him that she was Joby's daughter because her words echoed what Joby had told him when they were together in his cabin.

'He's not just panning dust from a

stream,' she said, 'he's found a rich vein in the hills, which needs to be mined.'

By now the sky was pink and Wes was anxious to get back to the couple who called themselves Anne and Frank Morphy. He hurried the preparations of Gil and the woman he now believed to be Joby's daughter, but they were barely in their saddles before the sound of gunfire echoed down the hillside. Two shots, which set Wes Gray moving along the trail at a long-legged lope.

7

Confident that Gil Forbes was savvy enough not to rush pell-mell in the direction of the gunshots, that the girl's safety would be his first concern, Wes Gray left them to their own devices and set off with a long, rhythmical stride to cover the distance between the two camps. Caution had ever been his watchword, so much so that under such circumstances avoiding the recognized trail was an instinctive tactic. Instead, he sought out and used every available rock, tree and bush that obscured his progress, pausing only when he reached some concealing foliage, which provided an unobstructed view of the pair who called themselves Frank and Anne Morphy.

Anne sat on a rock like a penitent schoolgirl, her arms clasping her knees, her head bowed as it had been throughout the journey, her gaze on some indeterminate point a short distance ahead. Frank was pacing the area in which they'd camped, the pistol in his right hand pointing nowhere in particular. From time to time he looked at Anne but no word passed between them. Often his attention was focused on the higher ground, his lips forming a grimace of impatience, as though by now his gunshots should have brought some response. When, eventually, Gil Forbes and Anne Cowell hove into view, he couldn't disguise his surprise.

'Who's this?' he muttered and Anne Morphy raised her head to study the approaching riders.

Acutely aware of the scout's ability to cover ground quickly, Gil Forbes was surprised that there wasn't any sign of Wes Gray. He was also aware of the pistol held by the man in the middle of the trail and, although it was held at his side in a somewhat lackadaisical manner, the set of the man's features conveyed his willingness to use it if the need arose. When Gil reined his horse to a halt he was relieved to see Wes Gray step from cover behind the man; his rifle, held purposefully in both hands, was pointed at the middle of the armed man's back.

'Drop the gun.' Wes's words, delivered with a gruffness which indicated he would brook no dissent, startled Anne Morphy, who hadn't heard his approach even though he was now but a yard from her side.

Frank began to turn but Wes ordered him once more to drop the gun. Keeping his rifle trained on Frank he began to circle him, moving round towards Gil and Anne Cowell, coming slowly into Frank's range of vision. Frank began to put his gun in his side holster.

'I won't tell you again, Frank. Throw the gun away.'

This time, because he could see Wes Gray's face, Frank did what he was told, casting the revolver five or six yards to his right. 'What's this all about?' he asked.

'You tell me,' replied Wes. 'Why did you fire those shots?'

'We didn't know where you were. Thought perhaps you'd got lost and needed a signal to find your way back.'

Wes shook his head. The explanation didn't ring true. Since leaving Council Bluffs they'd taken precautions to keep their journey secret, and the closer they got to their destination the more important it became to maintain their vigilance. On the first night, he'd slept apart from Frank and Anne, keeping guard as they slept to ensure their safety. There was no reason to attach any different interpretation to his absence from the camp this morning.

Momentarily he turned his attention to Anne Morphy. She had barely moved during the interplay between himself and Frank; she still clasped her knees, but her wide-open eyes stared anxiously at Gil and Anne Cowell, as though she was aware that their arrival was an ill omen for her.

'If there are robbers in the neighbourhood those shots will probably bring them here in a hurry,' Wes said.

Once again a sly expression crossed Frank's face. He jerked his head in the direction of Gil Forbes and Anne Cowell. 'Who are these people?' he asked. 'Perhaps they are part of the robber band.'

Wes introduced the two riders. 'I've known Gil for years,' he informed Frank. 'He's been on our trail because the girl with him is the true daughter of Joby Patton.' He paused for several seconds, giving the news he'd imparted time to settle in the minds of those he had covered with his rifle. 'So,' he said eventually, 'who are you?'

Surprisingly, Frank didn't argue; the smirk remained in place, as though the whole enterprise had been a joke that Wes was late catching on to.

'Guess you've rumbled our little game,' he said. Spreading his arms wide, he added, 'Can't blame a man for trying to find the mother lode. Rumour

110

has it that the old man's made a rich strike. We figure there's probably enough gold in the ground to make more than one man rich. Once you'd led us to his workings we'd know where to set up our own operation. We weren't intending to rob anyone.'

'So who are you?' repeated Wes.

'Frank and Alice Morphy,' Frank replied, moving as he spoke towards the girl sitting a few yards away. 'Simple folk looking to make their fortune out west.' Wes motioned for him to stop with a jerk of his rifle. 'OK if I get some coffee?'

'Do it easy,' warned Wes, watching as Frank moved to where a coffee pot stood on hot stones. 'And you are his wife?' he asked Alice.

The girl appeared drained of all colour; her hands were now pressed against her cheeks as though anticipating severe consequences as a result of the revelation of the deception. Her eyes moved to Frank, who, having picked up the pot, now faced her, showing his back to the frontiersman.

When Wes repeated his question it seemed for a moment that Alice Morphy would reply, but before she was able to do so Frank lashed out with his left hand and struck her across the face with an open palm. She cried out, staggering to her feet to get away from him but he caught her by the arm and pulled her towards him.

'Stop,' ordered Wes, raising his rifle in a more threatening stance but instantly knowing that it was a futile gesture. He couldn't fire it because of the possibility of shooting the girl.

By now Frank was holding Alice in front of him, a shield against Wes's weapon. Instantly, Wes cast aside the rifle, took two steps forward, then flung himself at Frank. Frank's reaction was almost as quick. He pushed Alice to the ground and threw the coffee pot at the hurtling figure of the scout. The pot struck Wes's shoulder, the contents spread across his back but this was insufficient impediment to halt his attack. He collided with Frank, toppling him to the ground. For several seconds they rolled in the dust, each trying to gain dominance. Frank was the heavier man and no stranger to brawling and being victorious. He expected to emerge the winner from this struggle, too.

Wes Gray, however, was quick, strong and resourceful. Frank discovered that his weight counted for very little because every time he tried to pin Wes against the ground the frontiersman was able to squirm out of his clutches, then deliver blows to his head and body. They wrestled for several minutes, Wes gaining the upper hand, punishing Frank, inflicting a cut or bruise to his face with almost every punch.

Surprised by the ease with which Wes had proved the master, Frank sought some means of turning the tables. Secreted under his jacket, tight against his left side, he carried a knife in a soft leather scabbard. That, he knew, could give him the advantage he needed to win the fight, but first he had to escape Wes's continuous assault. His chance came as they rolled to and fro across the clearing. A confining circle made up of weighty stones had been formed for their breakfast fire. Summoning up his fast-dwindling strength, Frank closed his right hand around one of them. It was hot, painful to hold, but, if he was successful, it was a pain he needed to endure only for a few seconds. A solid, stunning strike against Wes Gray's skull would enable him to free himself and reach his knife.

Frank's ploy almost worked. For a moment he relaxed his struggle as though he was about to cede victory to his adversary, a manoeuvre which had worked for him in the past, but Wes Gray was experienced in the ways of barroom brawlers and although he, too, ceased his onslaught, willing to accept Frank's surrender if it was genuine, he was prepared when the other's right arm came swinging in a violent arc towards his head.

Instantly, he rolled to his right, keeping his head clear of the vicious blow. Instead, it glanced off the top of his left arm causing little pain to the frontiersman, and he scrambled out of range. Wes expected Frank to attack again with the rock but when he gained his feet he saw that Frank had cast aside that weapon and was brushing aside his jacket to display the haft of the knife, which was pouched on his left hip. Wes grinned, producing on his face an expression that brought fear to anyone who saw it.

Motionless, momentarily rooted to the spot with the knowledge that revealing his knife had played into his enemy's hands, Frank watched as Wes pulled his own Bowie knife from its sheath. Frank knew the tales of Wes Gray but until this moment had dismissed them as western folklore, doubting that the frontiersman was any more dangerous than any other man he'd faced. Now, however, separated by a handful of paces, seeing that awful, knowing expression on the other's face and the great curved blade in his hand, Frank knew he had been mistaken. Wes Gray was capable of killing him, was smiling at the prospect of such an act, knowing he was a better man with a knife than Frank could ever be.

Frank paused, watching as Wes used seemingly languid loops to shift his knife from hand to hand, as though each time it was in the air was an offered opportunity to launch an attack. Beads of sweat had begun to form on Frank's brow. He wondered how many men had already been killed by that knife and, if the tales of Wes Gray's Indian ways were true, how many scalps had been lifted from dead heads. Now Wes Gray had adopted a fighting crouch, was beckoning him forward, and like a fool, he went.

Rushing like a bull he charged, head down, hoping the impetus of his attack would catch Wes Gray unprepared, that his speed and weight would overpower him and in that moment of superiority he would be able to deliver a killing blow. If he could ground his opponent he was confident that the victory would be his, but sudden and swift though his charge was, he was the one who sprawled in the dirt and lay at the mercy of his adversary. One moment he was racing towards the broad target of Wes Gray's buckskin-covered chest and the next he was butting fresh air, the scout having stepped aside to avoid the collision.

As Frank passed by, Wes kicked his legs out from under him. Grunting with pain and surprise Frank crashed on to the rock-hard surface. Instantly Wes took command, kicking away Frank's knife and dropping on top of him, driving the remainder of the air from his body. He pressed his Bowie knife against Frank's throat, its point so sharp that it slit the skin and a droplet of blood bubbled out. Frank's eyes bulged in their sockets. These, he was sure, were his last seconds of life.

But Wes had no intention of killing him at that moment. He wanted information from him, wanted to know the details of his scheme and the names of any confederates, He also wanted to know if Frank had been part of the gang that had stolen his pelts and, if so, where the other members of that gang could be found. He pressed the point of his knife at another part of Frank's neck, producing another pinprick of blood. It was a hint to Frank that Wes wanted answers to the questions he was about to ask. But the questions were never voiced.

Looming over Frank, their faces almost touching, Wes Gray imparted the silent message that he was the victor, that total obedience was Frank's only hope of survival. But even as Frank's capitulation showed in the dullness of his eyes and the sag of his flesh a shout came from Gil Forbes, a warning which was cut short by a gunshot, a woman's cry of alarm and the ungraceful sounds of a startled horse. Wes raised his head. Legs in black trousers were approaching and the butt of a rifle was swinging in a dreadful arc towards his head. Unable to prevent it, the wooden stock smashed against his temple and, unconscious, he rolled on to his back.

Later, when Wes tried to move, the blurred vision which had been the most prominent aspect of his returning senses was quickly replaced by dizziness and a savage pain in his head. Unintentionally, indeed unwittingly, he emitted a low moan as he tried to struggle into a sitting position. This wasn't easy, not just because of the head blow he'd taken but because his legs and hands were now tied. He rested a moment, prayed that his return to consciousness had not yet been discovered so that he could get a grasp on the events that had led to this situation. He closed his eyes, hoping that when he reopened them his vision would have cleared.

Alice Morphy was the first person on

whom he focused clearly. She was half a dozen yards away, sitting with her back against a high boulder, looking directly at him, her eyes wide as though she had become lost in a strange and dangerous land and was hoping that he knew the route to safety.

Further along from Alice, Anne Cowell was on her knees, her back to Wes, her attention completely given to whatever lay on the ground beyond. The memory of the warning cry and the sounds that had accompanied it before he had been struck came to Wes. There had been a gunshot and Wes knew instantly that the object of Anne Cowell's concern was Gil Forbes. He struggled to sit up, tried to ignore the spasm of pain, the nausea and the vision-impairing flashes of colour, but was forced to sink back to the ground again to let the moment pass. His next attempt was more successful but by the time he'd shuffled into a sitting position with his back against a boulder he'd attracted the attention of his captors.

The man who had hit him approached. He was tall and the lower part of his face was covered with stubble that had grown for at least three days. His eyes were narrow as if he was permanently squinting against a bright sun. His clothes were black; black trousers, black shirt, black hat and a short black jacket. He held his rifle by the end of the barrel while the butt rested on the ground. Wes could see stains on it which, he guessed, were made by his blood.

'So,' the man said, 'the famous Wes Gray.' He didn't speak again for several moments, merely looked down at his prisoner as though savouring the position in which he found himself. 'When you're ready,' he continued, 'you can finish your journey.'

Wes turned his head to look where Anne Cowell nursed Gil Forbes. 'How bad is he?' he asked.

The man grinned as if to say, *Does it matter?* but satisfied himself by giving no answer to Wes's question, asking instead one of his own. 'Joby Patton, where is he?'

Wes defied him. 'Couldn't tell you,' he said.

By now the man in black had been joined by Frank Morphy and two other men. It was Frank who spoke, edging forward in a menacing manner, a scowl on his face and his hand seeking the hilt of his knife.

'I'll make him talk.'

'No need for that,' said the man in black. 'He'll take us there.' He took two steps to where Anne Cowell still knelt on the ground, grabbed her arm and pulled her to her feet. Anne struggled but when he placed the barrel of his gun at her temple she subsided. 'This is the old man's daughter. What do you think he'll value most? The gold or his daughter?'

Wes knew the answer to that but he also knew that once he led the robbers to Joby's cabin they would all be killed. Still, if he refused to lead them they wouldn't get any further than this campsite and if they found the deeds that Anne was carrying they would know where to find Joby.

'Let me look at Gil,' Wes said. 'When he's able to travel I'll take you.' It was in his mind to play for time. Perhaps between here and Joby's cabin he'd get the chance to turn the tables on the robbers.

8

Released from his bindings, Wes inspected the bullet wound in Gil's shoulder. It was ugly but, if properly treated to prevent poisoning of his system, not life-threatening. Wes suspected that the bone had been broken or chipped and would be causing immense pain but Caleb Dodge's right-hand man was gritting his teeth and trying not to show it. While Wes examined the wound Anne Cowell, who had been at Gil's side from the moment he hit the ground, related the brief details of their capture.

'They didn't show themselves until it was clear that you had the upper hand in the fight,' she told Wes. 'When they emerged from their hiding-places they had their guns in their hands. Gil shouted a warning and went for his gun because he thought they were going to kill you. The man in black shot Gil before clubbing you.'

'I don't think killing me is part of their plan at the moment. They need me to take them to your father.' He cast a quick glance over his shoulder to where the four robbers were in a huddle, seemingly uncaring about the behaviour of their captives but Wes knew that they would be watchful of his every move. 'You mustn't let them know you have the deeds to the mine with you,' he whispered. 'If they get their hands on those they'll no longer need to search for your father.'

Anne nodded, acutely aware that the discovery of her father's papers would almost certainly result in death for herself, Wes and Gil. She looked to her left where Alice sat alone, pale and bemused. 'Who is she?' asked Anne Cowell.

'Fooled me into thinking she was you. Reckon she's part of the gang hoping to get your father's gold.'

'She hasn't spoken a word,' Anne

told him, 'and they've ignored her.'

Wes decided it was time to find out more about the girl who'd claimed to be Joby Patton's daughter. He collected some bandages from one of the packs they'd brought from Council Bluffs and asked Alice to assist while they tended to Gil's wound. Her presence was superfluous but he questioned her in a low voice while they worked on Gil's shoulder.

Her name wasn't Morphy and she wasn't Frank's wife. Her name was Alice Spencer and she'd arrived in town with her husband, Henry, during the period that Wes had been scouring the rooming houses for Joby's daughter. They were Mike Riordan's missing artists, not a song-and-dance routine but actors who performed popular scenes from Shakespeare's plays. They had been kidnapped and taken to a farmhouse where Henry Spencer was still held. Alice had been coerced into the role of Anne Patton to safeguard her husband's life and with the promise that they would be reunited when she returned to Council Bluffs.

Wes knew that that promise was worthless. When Frank Morphy found Joby Patton he would kill him and Alice would be a witness to the slaying. She would never be allowed to return to Council Bluffs and it was possible that her husband was already dead. Wes kept that thought to himself and supplied her with his own promise that he would do what he could to get her away from the robbers. It was a promise he intended to keep but at that moment he had no idea how. He had no plan in mind and no weapon to help him overcome his captors.

The man in black approached and stood over them while Anne Cowell tied the last knot to hold in place the padding which had been applied to stanch the flow of blood. 'Looks bad,' he said.

'He can't travel yet,' said Wes, hoping to delay their departure as long as possible, to give himself more time to work out a strategy to effect their escape.

The other nodded as though concern for Gil's welfare was a priority. 'I agree,' he said, 'but there's no need for him to go anywhere. Old Man Patton won't be expecting anyone other than you and his daughter. Steve and Ben will stay with those two,' he indicated Gil and Alice Spencer, 'until we return.'

Wes stood upright, looking into the man's eyes, wanting to argue against the proposal but knowing that it would do no good. The man rested his right hand on the handle of his pistol, making it clear that he would have his way.

'Johnny Stoltz,' Wes said, naming the man he faced, making it clear that even though he was unarmed he didn't fear him, 'you stole my pelts. I mean to get the money I'm due.'

If Johnny Stoltz was surprised by the voicing of his name or by Wes Gray's declared intention it was clear that neither gave him cause for concern.

'Perhaps we'll discuss it when we reach the old man's cabin,' he said, 'but for now,' he continued, 'you and the girl saddle up. Sooner we get there the sooner we get everything sorted.' He turned and walked away, crossed the clearing to where one of the other men stood with the robbers' horses, which had been left to graze close by.

Alice Spencer's anxiety at the prospect of being left behind was clear to see. Wes's assurance that he would be back for her did little to allay her fears and her original belief that she and her husband would eventually be released unharmed was waning now with every passing minute. Wes Gray's earlier discovery of the deception had been a relief and a source of hope that all would be resolved before any harm befell Henry, but now the tables had been turned once more and she feared for her life. The faces of the two outlaws who were to be her guards displayed no sign of compassion; indeed they had thrown looks in her direction that made her uneasy, and she couldn't expect any protection from the wounded man, Gil Forbes. He could barely maintain consciousness and was tormented by pain with every movement.

Wes clearly saw Alice's fear in her wide-eyed expression and although he'd offered words that were meant to assure her that all would be well he knew that they had no true foundation but sprang merely from self-belief. At present he had no notion of what could be done to save or protect her; all he could do was head up the trail with Anne Cowell and hope for an opportunity to escape their captors.

Wes and Anne were in the lead when the foursome set out. Frank rode with his rifle resting across his knees but Johnny seemed dismissive of any notion that they might attempt to escape. Wes cast a glance behind at Gil and Alice and prayed that he wouldn't hear pistol shots resounding across the hillside as they moved further away.

Joby Patton's cabin wasn't too far

from the campsite. Wes had planned it that way, not wanting to arrive in the darkness of the previous night in case the prospector mistook them for part of the robber gang. They had been travelling for no more than twenty minutes when they reached the part of the trail where Wes had found Joby. The debris of the landslide trap still littered that part of the trail, triggering in Wes's mind the recollection that Joby had set up other rock snares along the trail. The possibility of finding and using one to foil Johnny Stoltz a second time appealed to Wes. Throwing a swift glance over his shoulder he could see that Johnny, too, remembered this place, was probably recalling how close he'd been to being swept off the hillside, or perhaps wondering how Joby had survived the avalanche.

They moved on. Wes manoeuvred his mount closer to Anne's and spoke in a low voice. 'If I yell,' he said, 'get your head down, give that horse a kick and ride away as fast as he'll go.'

She turned to look at him, wanted to ask if he had a plan, but a voice from behind brought to an end any conversation between them.

'If you're planning to make a break I'll blow you out of that saddle,' said Frank.

Wes twisted around. Their guards were half a dozen paces behind and Frank now had the butt of his rifle resting on his thigh, with his finger inside the trigger guard. 'The trail gets more difficult from here,' he called to Frank and Johnny, implying that Anne didn't spend a lot of time around horses and he wanted to be sure that she could cope with what lay ahead. To Anne he murmured, 'They won't shoot. Not while they think we're taking them to your father.' After a few strides he added, 'I'm more worried about Alice and Gil.'

'Me, too,' she replied.

They rode on in silence, Wes furtively scanning the trail ahead for another of Joby's rock traps but finding nothing.

By this time they were very close to the ravine off which lay the dry-bed gorge in which Joby's cabin was situated. Wes's mind was occupied not only with finding a means of escape for himself and Anne but also with issuing a warning for Joby.

The early-morning chill had long since vanished and even though they'd climbed higher up the hill-side the day was becoming hot. Ahead stood a defiant cottonwood; the spread of its spring-leafed branches cast a rare area of shade across the trail. When they reached it Wes drew his horse to a halt and Anne circled in beside him. He unhooked the water canteen that hung from his saddle horn and passed it to Anne.

'Who said to stop?' asked Johnny Stoltz.

'It's hot and dusty,' said Wes.

'You're part Sioux, aren't you?' said Frank. 'Heard that you people can travel all day without rest.'

Wes chose to ignore the inaccuracies

in Frank's comments. 'The lady needs a drink,' he said, although the true reason for halting was the hope that he could somehow use the properties of the low-hanging branches to dislodge his captors from their horses. If he could draw back a bough and let it swing forward at the appropriate moment it might provide an opportunity for escape. It was a long shot but he had to try something.

Johnny Stoltz didn't argue with Wes's stated reason, merely watched as Anne swallowed from the canteen, then dampened the bandanna she wore around her neck and replaced it. 'How much further?' he asked.

'We're getting closer.'

Johnny scowled at Wes's unhelpful answer. As he looked back down the trail to the place where he'd had the earlier run-in with the prospector he muttered to himself, 'His cabin can't be far away.' Then he turned his attention back to Wes. 'Move on,' he commanded.

Wes decided that this was the moment to gamble. He wasn't holding any aces, it was all a matter of bluff, but they were too close to the gorge to delay longer and it was unlikely that there would be a better opportunity. Anne had turned her animal, had taken the initiative and was a handful of strides ahead. Frank had drawn level with Wes, his eyes following Anne's progress, his rifle once more lying across his lap. Johnny Stoltz, Wes hoped, was within the scope of the branch's arc when he released it.

If Wes's plan was to have any hope of success then surprise would be a key element. With that in mind, his first move was almost languid in its execution, moving his mount unhurriedly as though accepting the situation and following Anne's lead. Surreptitiously, however, he held on to a springy branch, dragged it with him as he made his way around the tree, priming it for a sharp recoil. Then he made his bid for freedom, the attack consisting of three separate actions.

At the moment he released the taut branch he spurred his horse forward, driving it into the side of Frank's mount, causing it to stumble and tumble, unseating Frank in the process amid a string of angry oaths. Meanwhile, the branch sprang forward in a rising arc, striking Johnny Stoltz and his horse, causing greater confusion than Wes could have expected. At one point it seemed that Johnny too would become separated from his mount; however, after several moments, Johnny gained control of the beast.

Meanwhile Wes executed the third part of his plan, yelling for Anne to ride hard. He, too, not wasting time by assessing the confusion he'd caused, put spur to his horse's flanks and followed her along the trail. Fifty yards ahead, their route veered around the hillside and once they'd attained that point they would be out of sight of Johnny and Frank. After that it was only a short dash into the gorge and with luck they could be into the concealed ravine undetected by their pursuers.

Frank Morphy cursed his horse for falling and for its awkward attempts to rise. He'd fallen heavily on his right shoulder, leaving a sharp pain as accompaniment to each movement of the corresponding arm. His first thought was to grab his rifle and throw lead at the fleeing riders but his rifle had slithered away and he found himself separated from it by his spooked horse. He drew his revolver but it was obvious from the jarring pain that he wouldn't achieve any accuracy with it. He pulled and pushed at his horse's head to manoeuvre it across the trail so that he could reach his rifle, and in so doing he pulled the horse into the path of Johnny Stoltz, his clumsiness earning a roar of anger. Ignoring Johnny's ire he retrieved his rifle and instantly put it to his shoulder. Disregarding the ache he sighted and fired.

By now Anne Cowell had reached the

sanctuary of the bend. Wes was of the firm opinion that, for the moment, Johnny Stoltz wouldn't try to kill him because he alone knew the location of Joby Patton's cabin. Without him they would once again be chasing a phantom, depending on chance to find the prospector and his hoard. Even so, as he rode in Anne's wake he stretched his body along his horse's neck so as to present the smallest target possible to those behind.

Frank fired two shots before Johnny's angry command to stop firing penetrated. The first flew close to Wes, zinging through the air as it passed inches over his right shoulder. The second was aimed lower and found a mark. It wasn't Wes who was hit, it was his horse. The bullet struck the beast behind the saddle and travelled internally to puncture a lung. Its front legs buckled and as it fell it pitched Wes forward on to the hard rock trail. Momentarily winded, he lay listening to the animal's pain-filled breathing.

The instinct for survival brought him to his feet. Up ahead he could see that Anne Cowell had reined her mount to a halt, was turning its head in preparation for returning to his assistance. He waved her away with forceful gestures. Even if she failed to find her father she was safer free from the clutches of the robbers. He had no doubt in his ability to track her when he'd settled his business with Johnny Stoltz and Frank Morphy.

Johnny was fast approaching; he had his pistol in his hand but Wes knew that at this time it was little more than a demonstration of power. He'd heard the instruction for Frank to cease fire so there was little chance that he would shoot Wes: at least, not to kill.

Lithely, Wes stepped off the trail, slipped between two boulders, crouching low as he moved and weaved between stones, following a course which took him further away from Johnny, hoping to confuse him, knowing that afoot the robbers were no match for him. He could move more quickly and quietly than they and he could use the cover of rocks and foliage to better effect. If Johnny and Frank dismounted and followed him among the boulders he would swiftly conquer them.

Wes climbed to the top of a flat-topped rock and watched Johnny's approach. He was surprised that his pace wasn't slackening, that he wasn't preparing to dismount. It could only mean that Johnny intended catching Anne Cowell. That wasn't in Wes's plan. With Anne free, with only his own safety to consider, he had greater scope to combat the robbers. His immediate reaction was to cause a diversion, prevent Johnny from going any further.

Atop the rock on which he lay there were a handful of loose stones. Wes gathered a couple, weighed them in his hand and prayed that they were big enough to cause some damage to Johnny. As he drew level Wes sprang to his feet and hurled the first stone. It hit the man in black on the chest and he'd barely realized what had struck him before the second one struck his jaw, cutting him and drawing blood.

With a yell, Johnny yanked the reins, pulling back the head of his beast, stopping it instantly, causing it to rear in a startled fashion. Wes threw a third rock, this one striking the animal on its underbelly, slashing it as though stabbed by a cruel, sharp rowel and it shrieked and plunged its forefeet to the ground with juddering force. Johnny barely hung on. In his anger he fired his gun but Wes was no longer in the place from which he'd launched the rocks. Before he had full control of his mount Wes was before him, on the trail, throwing his arms in the air in front of the horse's face, spooking it so that once more it reared and stamped, and Johnny was thrown from the saddle.

On impact with the ground his pistol was jerked from his hand, an event which didn't escape the notice of Wes

Gray. He moved for the weapon but so did Johnny Stoltz. Johnny lived by the gun. Day and night he was armed. A gun was the necessity of his life. He was closer to the weapon than Wes and moved more quickly than the frontiersman expected. As his arm snaked towards the handle Wes kicked him in the stomach. Johnny's reach was halted, he folded in on himself but the setback was short-lived. As Wes strode towards the revolver Johnny grabbed his leg and pulled him down. Wes grunted, surprised at the outlaw's power of recovery, but he swung his fist and smashed a blow against Johnny's jaw. Stunned, Johnny could do nothing to prevent Wes reaching the pistol but as he bent to pick it up a coil of rope fell over his shoulders and he was yanked off his feet.

Frank Morphy pulled the rope so tight that it burned the skin through Wes's buckskin shirt.

'I reckon it's time for you to lead us to the gold,' Frank said.

9

As a boy, Frank Morphy had been taller and broader than every other boy in his neighbourhood, and working in lumber mills and mines had filled out that early frame into the burly, heavily muscled man who now had Wes Gray at his mercy. His strength, and his willingness to demonstrate it on any man who opposed him, gave him a status among the people with whom he now rode. So as not to incur his anger, they listened to him when he spoke, but mainly they agreed with him and did his bidding only because they feared his fists.

In his own mind, however, this subservience made him a leader, perhaps not the boss but one whose opinion mattered and who had the right to act in accordance with his own judgement. He did recognize authority, did know that the boss-man was smarter and that Johnny Stoltz's ability with a six-gun gave him precedence in the gang, but it didn't stop him testing the limit of his own importance or even acting against an order if he thought he had the right to do so. Such was his reasoning now, with Wes Gray roped and helpless on the ground at his feet.

Frank's face still smarted from the punches Wes had landed but worse than that, he recalled the fear that had gripped him when the point of Wes's Bowie knife had been pressed against his throat. He had had no doubt that he was about to die. He had never seen such a cold expression of savagery on anyone's face as that which had been on Wes Gray's. He was convinced that Wes had intended to inflict a hideous death on him and he had been almost paralyzed with fear. Other men had bettered him in fist fights in the past and all had later paid for it with their lives. He saw no reason why Wes Gray should be any different.

Putting all his weight into a kick,

Frank drove his leather-booted right foot at Wes Gray's midriff. Wes, recalling the oft-present smirk he'd seen on Frank's face, expected such a move. It was the look of a man who enjoyed having the upper hand and dishing out violence. Frank was a bully who would take every advantage available to him. Accordingly, Wes did his best to ride the blow, lifting his stomach and rolling away from the kick, reducing the force of the impact although not averting altogether its power and resulting pain.

Bending, Frank took hold of the rope which still encircled the frontiersman's body and pulled forcefully, lifting Wes's shoulders and head off the ground. Grasping the rope in his left hand he hauled on it as he delivered a right-hand punch to the side of Wes's head, making it impossible for him to avoid the full force of the blow. He repeated the action, cursing as he did so and promising Wes a long and painful death.

Slapping the dust from his clothes,

Johnny Stoltz got to his feet and gingerly touched the area where Wes's boot had landed. 'That's enough,' he shouted. Even though he, too, possessed thoughts of vengeance he knew they had to wait. They'd been fortunate to avert Wes Gray's escape plan and fortunate, too, that the shot he'd fired in a moment of blind self-preservation had not killed him. There would be time enough for revenge when they got from their prisoner the information they sought.

Frank Morphy threw another punch at Wes, hitting him so hard that he had to let go of the rope and let the scout drop once more to the ground.

'That's enough,' repeated Johnny Stoltz, who could see the glint of murder in the other's eyes. 'We still need him.'

For a moment it seemed that Frank's temper would not be assuaged by Johnny's words. He reached forward as if to grab Wes's buckskin shirt, but when he glanced at Johnny he paused, then drew back. Johnny had his hand on the butt of his pistol and an ice-cold look on his face. Frank had seen that expression several times in the past and knew that it held no goodwill for the person at whom it was aimed. Johnny Stoltz's drawing speed meant that Frank had now reached the limit of his authority.

'When we find the prospector I want the pleasure of killing this one.' Frank emphasized his words by thrusting his boot at Wes.

Johnny paid no heed to the other's words; instead he made an arm movement which indicated that he wanted Frank to step away from Wes.

Wes looked up; his lip was cut and a bruise was developing along the left side of his jaw. 'What makes you think I'll take you any further?' he asked. 'The girl's gone. If I arrive at the old man's cabin without her and with you in tow he's likely to shoot all three of us.'

Frank said, 'In that case we'll revert

to our original plan. I'll bring the actress up here and we'll use her to get into the old man's cabin.'

Wes poured scorn on Frank's scheme. 'I think Joby knows his daughter. And,' he added, 'I don't think he's too fussy about shooting women if his gold is threatened.'

'The girl,' Johnny mused, looking up the trail in the direction in which Anne Cowell had ridden. 'I doubt if she's too far ahead. Probably waiting for this Indian-lover to catch up.'

Frank agreed. 'Didn't seem like much of a horse-woman. Ought to be able to find her if we keep going.'

'You go and find her. One horse on her trail and she might show herself. If she hears three she'll know his escape plan failed.'

Frank considered the order as if Johnny might be hatching some plan to get rid of him but, eventually, he agreed. He unlooped his rope from around Wes, then secured his hands behind his back with a long strip of leather that he found in a saddle-bag.

'If you hurt that girl I'll kill you when you return,' Wes told him.

Frank paused, taken aback by the confidence in Wes's voice, talking as though he was the captor not the captive. The sooner they found the old man and his gold strike the better Frank would like it. Despite the fact that they had Wes Gray at their mercy, Frank wouldn't be easy until he'd plugged the frontiersman with every bullet in his pistol. Frank wanted him dead, wanted to quell the ferocity that showed in the other's eyes, wanted to shake off the overpowering sense that Wes Gray had the ability to reverse the situation and when he did his retribution would not bring about a swift death. He put his hands on Wes's chest and pushed him violently. Wes overbalanced and crashed against the hard rock of the hillside.

As Frank rode away, Johnny Stoltz chuckled. It wasn't a laugh of mirth, more an expression of contempt for his companion. 'You've got Frank jumping like a pronghorn that's sniffed a grizzly,' he told Wes, who was sprawled half-stunned on the ground. When he didn't get a response, Johnny spoke again, kicking at Wes's feet as he did so, not only to command Wes's attention but also to demonstrate that, unlike Frank, he wasn't unnerved by his reputation. 'Don't know why I didn't wait until you'd slit his throat before clubbing you. His arms are strong enough but his brain is weak. He lacks the guts for a real fight. Someone like you, now, it would be an honour to ride with. You're not the sort to be scared by stories of another man's deeds. They would have to prove to you that they were the better man and I don't suppose there are many who can do that.'

Wes didn't respond but shuffled himself into a sitting position and leant back against the rock behind.

Johnny Stoltz squatted beside him, pushed his hat back off his brow and squinted against the brightness of the sun reflecting off the hard rock face. 'There's no need for you and me to be enemies,' he said. 'No need for anyone to get hurt. All we want is the gold. If the old man signs over his claim we'll leave him alone.'

'But it is his,' said Wes. 'He found it. He worked it out of the ground. He deserves it.'

Johnny laughed. 'You know as well as I do that that isn't sufficient reason for him to keep it. If you want it you've got to be strong enough to hold on to it.'

'That's what he's trying to do, what he's asked me to help him do.'

'What has he offered you?' asked Johnny Stoltz. 'How much of his gold will you get? Throw in with us and you'll get a share like everyone else.'

'That would put me on a level with Frank,' said Wes. 'Not much of an offer.'

Easy money had been the corner-stone of Johnny Stoltz's life and he assumed that every man was as susceptible as himself to its appeal, so he was content to believe that the scout saw his offer as a genuine inducement. Johnny, of course, had no more intention of sparing Wes's life than he had of allowing Joby Patton or his daughter to survive once he had his hands on the gold, and to achieve that he was happy enough to resort to trickery. 'Quite right,' he said. 'You deserve a greater reward. When we get back to Council Bluffs I'll speak up for you with the boss. He's a fair man. He'll see things my way.'

'The boss?'

'Yeah, sure. You'll meet him when we share out the gold. What do you say? Will you take us to the old man's claim?'

'There's something else we've got to sort out first,' said Wes. 'You stole my pelts. I want my money.'

For a moment Johnny Stoltz was as astounded by Wes Gray's confidence as Frank Morphy had been several minutes earlier. Then he laughed. 'Two hundred dollars,' he said. 'All they were worth was two hundred dollars.'

'But it's my two hundred dollars.' The words were spoken softly but the fire of anger that flashed from Wes's grey eyes carried such a message of hatred that Johnny Stoltz knew that the scout had no intention of leading the robbers to the miner. He jumped to his feet, drew his pistol, the thought going through his mind that he should kill his prisoner now, that he couldn't afford him the possibility of escape because, if free, he would have no mercy on those who had captured him.

At that moment, however, the report of a rifle shot echoed from higher up the hillside. Frank had caught up with Joby Patton's daughter. A look passed between Wes and Johnny, both of them knowing that this was the end of the trail if the girl had been killed.

Johnny broke the silence with one of his forced laughs. 'That'll be Frank's signal that he's caught the girl.' He stepped away from Wes, moved a little way up the trail as if in anticipation of Frank's immediate appearance, then returned to stand near his mount as though considering a sortie uphill to satisfy his curiosity.

Wes wasn't sure that Johnny believed his own statement, but they wouldn't know the truth until Frank returned. He rested back against the rock and spent the next few minutes in silence, splitting the focus of his attention between the trail ahead and Johnny Stoltz.

They heard the steady sound of shod hoofs on the hard rock moments before the rider came into view. Frank was alone, his horse moving slowly as though without purpose, its neck stretched forward as though searching the ground for grass to chew. But Frank wasn't showing any urgency either as he sat astride the dun gelding. His head was down on his chest as though he was sleeping and his big shoulders were slumped forward, giving the impression that he was folded at the waist.

Johnny called his name as he approached but got no response. He grabbed the horse's bridle, halted it abruptly, causing Frank to pitch out of the saddle and land heavily on the ground. It was immediately clear that Frank was either dead or dying. There was an ugly hole in his chest and the front of his shirt was covered in blood. Surprised by this turn of events, Johnny knelt at Frank's side, seeking some clue as to how such a fate had befallen him. He hadn't accidently shot himself, the rifle still couched in the scabbard on Frank's horse ruled out such a mishap, and even if the girl was capable of such shooting, there had been only one shot; where had the weapon come from? She had been unarmed when making her dash for freedom so the shot must have been fired by someone else. The girl's father was the obvious candidate, which meant that his cabin and the gold were close at hand. He didn't have to hunt for Joby Patton any longer, Joby Patton had found him.

Johnny's thoughts turned to Wes Gray. In these altered circumstances was his prisoner an asset or a liability? Could he bargain with the miner, the frontiersman's life for his gold mine? It seemed unlikely. Joby Patton knew that his own life and that of his daughter were forfeit the moment he signed over his claim. He would protect his fortune to the last moment. Wes Gray would simply become another casualty in the fight to hang on to the gold. So, he concluded, Wes Gray had to die. He couldn't rid himself of the sense of ferocity that the frontiersman exuded, even though he was bound and unarmed. He had to be killed and it needed to be done now. He dropped his hand to the butt of his pistol and began to rise. Then everything changed.

As he'd been taught by the Arapaho and Sioux people among whom he'd lived, Medicine Feather, Wes Gray, had learned to observe the land in which he travelled and harness its natural bounty for his own use. According to Joby

Patton, these hills concealed gold, but Wes had seen something more practical to the Indian tribes which could now help him to escape captivity. Here and there as they'd climbed he'd seen strata of obsidian rock, the hard stone with which the tribesmen made arrowheads, axe-heads, tools and other weapons. Sharp edges remained where chunks had previously been hewn from the surface.

Earlier, when Frank Morphy had tied his hands behind his back with the leather thong, he had goaded the big man into losing his temper, hoping he would be knocked to the ground, which might give him the opportunity to squirm his way to a suitable outcrop. His luck had been better than he'd hoped: Frank pushed him off balance so that he crashed into the hillside at the most advantageous spot. His right shoulder had taken the full impact of his fall but it hadn't hampered his ability to work his binding against a particularly sharp edge. Ever since

Frank had set off in pursuit of Anne Cowell, Wes had used that edge to saw through the leather strip. Now, with a final wrench, he was free.

At the other side of the clearing, with his back to Wes, Johnny knelt beside the body of Frank Morphy. Instantly, Wes was up and moving swiftly across the clearing in a crouched, silent run. Even though he was weaponless, it was Wes's intention to kill Johnny Stoltz; he would wrap his arm around his neck and crush his windpipe before Johnny had any chance to retaliate, but while yet three strides short of his target, Johnny began to rise, drawing his pistol as he did so.

With the circumstances altered it became necessary for Wes to revise his attack. He didn't underestimate Johnny Stoltz's prowess with a gun and therefore it was essential to disarm him. Before Johnny was aware that he was under threat, Wes hurled himself forward, crashing into the other with such force that the pistol fell from his hand. The gun spun and slithered across the rock and down the hillside and Johnny went full length as Wes landed his first blow. Johnny kicked out, his foot making contact with Wes's shin, scraping it but without any sort of impact to halt Wes's onslaught. The frontiersman swung a looping right-hand punch at Johnny Stoltz's head. Because the right-hand side of the robber's face was already pressed against the ground he couldn't avoid the blow and it smashed into his left cheek just below the eye. Swiftly, Wes was upon him trying to get his fingers around the other's throat, but Johnny Stoltz knew he was fighting for his life and was not prepared to let it go cheaply.

Producing a surprising burst of power, Johnny managed to bring his arms up between Wes's and thrust them aside, loosening the grip around his throat. He heaved his body upward, throwing aside Wes as a bucking bronco would an inexperienced wrangler. Again he kicked out, this time his hard leather boot made contact with Wes's buckskin-clad back. Wes grunted as he rolled away, then rose to one knee as he prepared to renew his attack.

Johnny Stoltz had gained a moment's respite but he had little confidence in achieving total victory. He was a gunman, unaccustomed to brawls; he knew that desperation was his current saviour. He scanned the area for a weapon, a rock, a lump of wood, anything that would give him an advantage over Wes Gray. There was a small rock, possibly one of those thrown at him earlier, which might be useful. A powerful strike with it, he reckoned, might set Wes Gray back on his heels long enough for him to reach the rifle on Frank's horse. In one fluid motion he picked up the rock and threw it, barely pausing after its release before making a dash for the rifle.

Wes reacted just as quickly, ducking under the rock and driving forward in an attempt to be first to the horse. It was a close contest, one which Johnny might have won because he approached the horse from the side where the rifle hung, but Wes, thinking quickly, rammed his shoulder into the horse's rear. It jumped and shied away from him, collided with Johnny and sent him sprawling across the ground.

Momentarily, the advantage belonged to Wes but that which seemed to have won him the day just as suddenly took it from him again. Perhaps the horse was already skittered by the smell of Frank Morphy's blood but it certainly didn't enjoy the whack it received from Wes, and it retaliated. Wes was about to lean over its back to grab the rifle when the beast swung its rear end back towards Wes and lashed out with its back legs.

Fortunately for Wes he was still a little to the side and he avoided the iron-shod hoofs, but still the power of the thrust lifted him across the ground. Scrambling to his feet he realized that Johnny Stoltz was just a few short strides from the horse. In a moment he would have the rifle and there was nothing Wes could do to stop him. Escaping with his life was the best he could achieve for the moment so he turned towards the high ground, found the shelter of a boulder, then crouched, rolled and ran in a zigzag manner as bullets pinged and ricocheted off the rocks around him.

Within moments he'd completely confused Johnny Stoltz, had changed direction so many times that the robber was barely sure if he'd gone up the trail or down.

10

If Wes Gray had expected Joby Patton to remain on his bunk until he returned from Council Bluffs he couldn't have been more wrong. Before leaving, he had knocked together two crude crutches to provide a little support when the old prospector needed to move around the cabin, but he had barely disappeared from view before Joby was making plans to give himself greater mobility. During his life the old man had been accused of many failings but idleness had never been one of them.

Protecting himself was of paramount importance and with his armoury enhanced by the guns Wes had retrieved from his hillside traps, he felt capable of resisting an attack on the cabin for some time. However, if his attackers chose to burn down the cabin, escape would be impossible. He needed to be able to travel beyond his cabin. His mule and the horse that had carried him back from the scene of the avalanche were grazing in an area behind the cabin. Although difficult and probably painful to execute, Joby didn't think it beyond his ability to harness one of them, but he knew that without help it would be impossible for him to mount either. The answer he came up with was a rugged travois, and he set about making one the day after Wes left for Council Bluffs.

It took him all day and many spasms of agony to complete the job. He scavenged the area around the cabin for any lengths of wood he could find, and with nails and rope created two spars of almost equal length. Then he created a mesh between them from the coils of thick rope he had stored in the cabin. He also created a rope harness with which he was able to attach the travois to the mule. By the end of the day he was exhausted and what he'd built looked insubstantial and unsafe, but Joby was satisfied that it would fulfil his needs until Wes returned with Anne.

The work had got him through the day, if not without pain then at least without the feeling of helplessness that lying on his bunk would have brought. The travois wasn't a work of art, it wasn't meant to be; it was for use in an emergency, one which he hoped would never arise because Wes and Anne would return within a couple of days.

The following day he experimented with the contraption, harnessed it to the mule and, lying on his stomach, guided it successfully up and down the ravine. It hadn't been easy, especially getting on to it and getting off again, but the hand-built bench that he kept at the side of the cabin had been useful at those times. The travois wasn't perfect, but he was sure it would fulfil the limited purpose for which it was intended.

He travelled further on it the next

morning, into the gorge, forcing himself to ignore the pain in his leg, careful to avoid as many bumps and rocks on the trail as possible but, being in the hill country, avoiding one obstacle often only put him in line with another.

He was halfway through the gorge, sweating and ready to turn back, when he heard the gunshot. He pulled the mule to a halt, debating with himself his next move and it was now that he realized the impracticality of his situation. A return to the cabin, while theoretically being his best course of action, was a non-starter. His progress was necessarily slow; he couldn't outpace anyone who saw him. In addition, lying face down without the facility to move quickly put him at their mercy. He had his rifle but he couldn't use it while trying to guide the mule and his accuracy with it would be non-existent due to the uneven surface over which he was travelling.

In the current circumstances a more sensible manoeuvre was to seek refuge behind a boulder or among some trees, where he'd be able to observe anyone who came along the trail. He'd head for home when all was quiet again. He began to turn, was square across the trail when the rider came in sight, travelling fast.

For a moment a collision seemed inevitable. Joby dropped the long rope he was using to guide the mule and the animal stopped instantly, blocking the trail. He reached for the rifle which, at the outset, he'd placed at his side but which, due to the judders of the journey, now lay trapped under his body. Joby's attempt to retrieve it was further hampered by its becoming ensnared in the rough fibres of the rope mesh. With one curse for his inability to gain command of the gun and another because of the pain of an ill-considered sudden movement, Joby awaited the oncoming rider, who was fast approaching.

Only a handful of strides separated them when the horse was pulled to a sharp halt, dust riding sharply from its skidding hoofs.

'Father,' called the rider, the word uttered both as an unsure question and a statement of joyful surprise. 'It's Anne,' she said, although the smile that was spreading across the old prospector's face made the self-identification unnecessary. Then she pointed back down the trail. 'Someone is chasing me,' she added. 'He means to kill me.'

Joby waved her aside, into the cover of a stand of trees. By now his rifle was grasped firmly in his hands. He waited and watched the approaching dot grow bigger until man and horse loomed large before him.

As Anne had done mere moments earlier, Frank Morphy pulled his horse to a halt a few yards short of the mule and travois which barred his path. It took but a moment for him to recognize Joby Patton and for a gleam of triumph to cross his face. He began to speak and his right hand moved towards his pistol, but Joby beat him on both counts.

'You're not killing anyone today,' he said, and pulled the trigger of his Winchester. The bullet smacked into Frank's abdomen, his left arm jerked, pulling the reins he held so that his horse turned until it was facing back down the hillside. Frank slumped, his head bowed as though inspecting the hole in his body, and the horse, urged by the spur pricks from Frank's death spasms, walked on.

'Was he alone?' Joby asked his daughter.

'No.' She summarized the events since leaving Council Bluffs. 'We should go and help Mr Gray,' she said in conclusion.

Joby shook his head. 'He doesn't need help from us. The best thing we can do is get back to my cabin. Wes'll come to us when he's able.'

No sooner had he finished speaking than more gunshots were heard, rapid firing but only the noise of one gun. They knew that Johnny Stoltz was the only one armed.

'Let's go,' urged Joby, insisting that there was no time for delay. 'If he's got the better of Wes he'll be coming after us.'

Reluctant though she was to abandon Wes and yet more anxious about Gil Forbes, she knew she couldn't forsake her father. He'd faced up to Frank Morphy for her, caught him unawares and killed him, but Johnny Stoltz, if he came after them, was now warned that they were close and dangerous. She had to get her father to the safety of his cabin.

It was decided that they would travel more quickly if Anne held the mule's bridle and guided it along the trail. With some difficulty, Joby was turned on to his back, which meant he could keep a lookout for signs of pursuit. He directed his daughter off the trail, told her to head for the left-side wall of the ravine. Not only would this lead them into the gorge where the cabin was, but it would hide them from the sight of anyone on their trail.

Even though it was uphill they made better time now than Joby had done during his awkward, painful outward journey. Although the less-travelled scrubland was even more rutted than the trail and caused Joby great jags of pain, he remained silent throughout.

They were less than a hundred yards from the entrance to the gorge and unaware that Johnny Stoltz had reached the entrance to the ravine when disaster struck. The makeshift travois proved too weak to withstand the constant buffeting from the bumps and crevices of the hillside. With Joby's downward weight competing against the upward thrust whenever the travois hit an obstacle there could be only one result: something had to give. It was the left-hand shaft. Bindings separated and those pieces of wood that were meant to be held together fell apart. Unable to prevent it, Joby rolled off with a dreadful yell.

Anne rushed to his side, retied the bindings in the hope that they would be able to cover the remaining distance without another mishap, and tried to get her father back on to the stretcher. For a few moments she struggled, finally realizing that he was too heavy for her to lift. She put her hands on her hips, gazed around in the hope that something would provide inspiration, and at that moment a gunshot split the air. Father and daughter exchanged worried looks. The shooter was close at hand, somewhere within the ravine.

★　★　★

Bemused by the speed with which he had lost track of Wes Gray's flight, Johnny Stoltz stood in the middle of the trail and slowly completed a full circle as he scoured the area for another glimpse of his adversary. It was as though the frontiersman possessed some magical power that enabled him to disappear at will. The moment Wes Gray had been flung across the mountain track Johnny had made a beeline for Frank's rifle, but by the time he'd pulled it from its scabbard Wes had gained his feet and raced to the cover provided by the rocks and gullies of the hills.

Johnny had given chase and when he caught sight of Wes's legs as he dived behind a low rock he'd fired two shots, but when he reached that point, expecting to finish off his unarmed adversary, he found no indication that he'd even been there. There seemed to be few places in the vicinity for a full-grown man to hide but Johnny hadn't seen Wes again.

Up high, Wes Gray squatted in the shadow cast by a huge overhang. His sure-footed progress from the trail below had been made easy because of Johnny Stoltz's ineptitude. It was clear to Wes that the gunman was bereft of all tracking skills and, as a fighter, depended solely on his ability with a gun. Perhaps if he'd had a clear sight of his quarry that marksmanship would have been decisive, but without a target he'd stumbled around with such clumsiness that his location had always been apparent to Wes Gray.

Wes had moved swiftly and silently whenever Johnny's gaze had been fixed in another direction and had had no trouble finding suitable niches, rocks and shrubbery as aids to his escape. Twice he had been within a few feet of his pursuer, lying in depressions that were just barely deep enough to obscure him, but his stillness and the camouflage of his buckskin clothing were sufficient for him to go unobserved.

It had crossed his mind on those occasions that it might be possible to surprise and overpower Johnny Stoltz, but he'd tempered his desire to conquer the robber with his awareness of Johnny's reputation with a gun. An unnecessary risk could be fatal not only for himself but for Joby and his daughter and for Gil Forbes and Alice Spencer, too. Now he watched, as Johnny prepared for his next move, knowing he would need to travel quickly if he was to provide protection for his friends.

Whatever Johnny chose to do, whether he rode on in the hope of finding Joby's cabin or turned back to rejoin the men he'd left guarding Gil and Alice, Wes knew that violence had to mark the end of his journey. In the belief that he was the most ruthless man in the territory, Johnny Stoltz would never stop in his pursuit of Joby Patton's gold.

At that moment, as he climbed into the saddle, Johnny was indeed considering which way he would ride. Frank Morphy's killing made it clear that someone else was close at hand. Joby Patton was the obvious candidate and capturing that old man's gold was his purpose for being in the hills at this time. The question was whether or not he needed the help of Steve and Ben to find him.

His deliberations lasted only a few moments. Frank Morphy might have got himself killed but he, Johnny Stoltz, was more than a match for a crusty old prospector. Besides, the shooting had taken place not far beyond that bend in the trail. If he moved quickly he might catch the old man before he hid himself away in whichever secret ravine he'd made his home. He kicked at his horse's flanks and headed up the trail.

As soon as Johnny kicked his horse forward, Wes abandoned the shadows and began running. For now, he believed he had two advantages over Johnny Stoltz: finding Joby had become the robber's top priority thereby lessening his watchfulness for the frontiersman, and, unlike Johnny, Wes knew the location of the miner's cabin.

Wes rounded the outcrop under which he'd held vigil and scanned the ravine which now lay below. It was narrow, steep-sided and stretched for half a mile, its entire length decorated with scattered patches of shrubbery and stands of trees. The dry-bed gorge in

176

which Joby Patton had built his cabin lay just beyond halfway. Further ahead, the other side of the ridge on which he now stood led down to Joby's cabin. There he would rearm himself, thus enabling him to confront Johnny Stoltz on equal terms. A look in the opposite direction showed him that Johnny Stoltz had reached the head of the ravine, where he'd halted to examine the trail ahead.

It was clear to the robber that the ravine presented plenty of suitable spots for a man to lie in ambush. He suspected that Frank Morphy's killer had fired from a clump of trees and could be hidden among them yet. He drew his rifle, rested the butt on his thigh and moved forward at walking pace. He cast looks right and left and sometimes up to the high ground but saw nothing. Instinct told him that he was close to discovering Joby Patton and his gold.

Wes Gray was confident that Johnny Stoltz wouldn't discover Joby's cabin and that when the robber had ridden beyond the ravine it would leave him plenty of time to fulfil his own plan. Like Johnny Stoltz, Wes had no doubt that Joby was responsible for the slaying of Frank Morphy, although how he'd overcome the handicap of a broken leg to get this far from the cabin nagged at his mind. The fate of Anne Cowell was also a matter for concern. Wes wondered if she was with her father or if she was still riding hell for leather towards the southern plains.

That question was answered as he began to make headway along the ridge. Movement, thirty feet below on the floor of the ravine, caught his attention and brought him once more to a standstill. They were about 400 yards ahead: a horse and an ass and two people who, at first observation, appeared to be locked in a struggle, each with their arms clasped over the other's shoulders and around the neck. One was on the ground, apparently at the mercy of the other, his head and body obscured by the torso of the other, his legs stretched straight and still. Then they shifted apart, the one on top standing tall, looking down on the other, hands on hips, considering the next move. That was when Wes realized that the one on the ground was Joby Patton and that it was his daughter, Anne Cowell, who stood over him.

For the moment, Anne and her father were obscured from Johnny Stoltz's vision by the occasional trees between but it was apparent that either sound or sight would soon make him aware of their presence. He was moving slowly, casting round as he rode for any sign that would lead him to those he sought. Wes knew he had to prevent their discovery for Johnny Stoltz would show no mercy to the miner and his daughter.

Another brief glance ahead showed Wes that the girl was striving to get her father to his feet. With the aid of a stick he was trying to stand but his broken leg was making it a difficult task. When

Wes realized that the stick was, in fact, a rifle, it gave him some hope that the miner would be able to defend himself when they were spotted. He searched for some means of sending a warning, letting them know that Johnny Stoltz was nearby, but nothing presented itself. The only means at his disposal was to throw a rock but the distance was too great and such an act was more likely to alert Johnny Stoltz that his quarry was close at hand than to raise a suitable alarm for his friends.

Without any other option, Wes Gray had to put himself in danger. By making his own presence known to Johnny Stoltz he might be able to draw him away from the others; if he could get him to shoot his rifle it would pinpoint his position, give Joby and his daughter the opportunity to protect themselves if his efforts failed.

For now, though, he was too far away from his enemy. Distracting him from his hunt for Joby and Anne wasn't sufficient; Johnny Stoltz would be relentless in his quest to get the old man's gold and Wes knew that nothing less than the death of his adversary would put an end to the pursuit. As he began his descent he had no idea how he would achieve such an outcome.

Johnny Stoltz hadn't increased his pace; he still moved at a sedate walk, his rifle ready and resting on his right thigh, his eyes scouring the terrain ahead, watching for dust in the air or hoofprints on the ground. He looked at the skyline on both sides of the ravine but only at what lay ahead. If he had turned his head to a greater degree he might have picked up the dust kicked up by Wes's rapid downward journey, but he didn't. Wes was behind him and moving quickly.

He was twenty yards behind and to the left of Johnny Stoltz when he shouted, whooping like a Sioux raider distracting Crow guards. Before the sound had died on his lips he had dived to his right, rolling behind a chosen boulder, then rising up and running at a crouch. Johnny was looking the wrong way, twisted in his saddle looking to his left and his rear, his rifle raised, a finger on the trigger.

A group of pines provided refuge for Wes. From among them he shouted again, dropping to the ground as Johnny swung his shoulders around and fired a shot into the timber cluster behind. Now there was stillness and Johnny wasn't sure if that was where the call had been made. Swiftly, he turned to his left again, suspecting that Wes had crossed behind once more, but there was no one there.

Behind Johnny's back Wes threw a rock forward, producing a smacking sound not unlike the report of a small handgun. Johnny reacted in the way Wes expected, firing once, twice and thrice in quick succession, each shot wasted as it thudded against hard rocks. While he was firing Wes recrossed the trail, flinging himself flat on the ground, waiting a moment to assure himself that Johnny wasn't looking in his direction before moving again.

Again he found sanctuary in a stand of pine trees. When he did it revived some knowledge, gave him a nucleus around which he could form a plan. He cast a look at Johnny, whose concentration still seemed to be focused to his right, towards the point where his last shots had been directed. Wes didn't know how many bullets the rifle still held, couldn't remember how many had been fired nor did he know whether Johnny had replaced those that he'd fired earlier. If not, there were probably no more than three in the magazine.

Wes picked out another point of cover: three large boulders long embedded where they stood and abutting each other like drunken cowhands at a bar. He weighed another rock in his hand, choosing a moment and a direction in which to throw that would result in more wasted bullets fired from Johnny's rifle. But Johnny acted first, surprising Wes by dismounting and treading cautiously away towards the spot where he thought Wes was hiding. This was a break that Wes hadn't expected but one which he gladly accepted.

With each step that Johnny took away from his horse, Wes crept a bit closer, staying close to the ground, watching Johnny's progress under the belly of the mount. Suddenly, as though his enemy had presented himself as an open target, Johnny wasted three more shots among the trees. While the echo of the reports still filled the air, Wes made his move. Reaching the animal he gathered up the reins, swung his right leg over the rump of the horse and clung on to the saddle, urging the horse forward, hanging along the flank so that he was hidden from Johnny's view. When he'd covered half a dozen strides he heard Johnny's shout of anger. After another half a dozen Wes swung up on to the saddle and gave another Indian whoop.

Johnny Stoltz raised his rifle and pressed the trigger. The hammer fell but the sound it produced was not what

Johnny expected. Instead of the explosion of gunpowder there was nothing but a hollow click. Again he tried and the gun produced the same result. The anger that had engulfed him when he realized that he'd lost his horse was inflated by the knowledge that his rifle was also useless to him. He flung it aside and drew his handgun, wanting to fire shots at the distant rider but knowing he was now out of range.

Looking back, Wes saw Johnny discard the rifle and for the first time that day he knew he had the upper hand. He reined the horse to a halt and dismounted.

'Come and get me,' he yelled at Johnny, then instantly moved into the trees to his left, knowing that in such an environment Johnny was out of his depth.

With his gun cocked and held before him, Johnny approached. Now and then he heard movement ahead, knocks against trees, twigs trampled underfoot, but he wasn't prepared to waste any bullets. His mind was full with thoughts of the retribution he would visit upon Wes Gray; he wouldn't be content with shooting him, he wanted him to suffer, wanted him to know the torment of pain. Another noise. Three trees away. It entered his mind to dodge off the trail after the next tree and circle round behind his enemy.

Wes Gray's memory had served him well and after issuing his challenge he'd worked his way back through the trees towards Johnny Stoltz. When he was in position he'd listened carefully for the sound of Johnny's approach; his heavy-booted tread. Johnny's dependence on his gun made him predictable, so Wes waited.

When the first crunch of rock crushed underfoot notified Wes of Johnny's nearness he threw a small stone at a tree further down the trail. Seconds later he threw a larger stone among some loose twigs. They crackled but again the sound was further away from Johnny than the point where Wes waited. When the shadow of Johnny's hat first edged into sight Wes threw another small pebble, again hitting a tree further ahead, luring Johnny into the belief that he had not yet reached his quarry. Wes watched the shadow as first it paused, then stepped on with greater confidence, heading straight for the tree behind which he waited. One more step, then he would strike.

Johnny Stoltz paused again, unable now to resist a boast of the advantage he imagined he held.

'I'm gonna drill you, Gray. You can run and hide but in the end I'll catch up. You're a dead man and so is that prospector when I find him.'

Holding his six-gun before him he stepped forward, but so sudden and unexpected was Wes Gray's strike that he was unable to discharge the weapon. Wes stepped forward, lunging, and the Cheyenne lance that had been one of Joby Patton's hideaway weapons went into Johnny Stoltz with such force that he was carried back a step before his knees folded under him and he sank on to his shins. Wes maintained the pressure, pushing the point clean through the other's body, pinning him, almost, to the rocky trail.

Johnny's gun had fallen from his hand, his face was contorted with agony, blood began to bubble from his lips.

'I am Medicine Feather,' said Wes, 'brother of the Arapaho, friend of the Sioux.'

Life was draining rapidly from Johnny when Wes leant closer. 'You should not have stolen my pelts,' he whispered.

11

There was less than fifty dollars in Johnny Stoltz's pockets, not a quarter of the amount that had been paid for Wes Gray's pelts, but Wes took the money along with the revolver that was lying on the ground. It wasn't that he wanted the gun but he needed something until he got his own back. He tucked the gun under his belt and walked away, leaving the skewered body in the middle of the trail, fodder for the wild animals of the hills.

Estimating the position in which he'd last seen Joby and his daughter, Wes made his way across the width of the ravine via a circular route, not approaching from the front lest an over-cautious Joby should shoot first and ask for identification afterwards. The gunshots, Wes guessed, would have put the old prospector on the defensive and he'd already killed one man this day to protect his daughter and his gold.

When he came across them Wes's guess proved accurate. Joby, prone on the ground and rifle tucked against his shoulder, was watching the land ahead, his narrow-eyed gaze scanning a vast arc of territory, determined that he wouldn't be surprised by anyone searching for them. Anne stood behind him, between their two animals, a hand over the muzzle of each to maintain silence.

Wes Gray spoke quietly as he emerged from the bushes on their right. 'No need for the rifle,' he said. 'Fighting's finished for the moment.'

The relief of both father and daughter was instantly apparent, the tense expressions on their faces falling away with their words of welcome. After telling them that Johnny Stoltz was dead, Wes expressed an urgency to get them back to the cabin.

'Gil Forbes and Alice Spencer are

being held by two of the gang back down the trail,' he told Joby. 'I need to get back there to help them.'

Joby had a pocket knife which Wes used to cut free the travois that was attached to the mule. Between them and without too much suffering or complaint from Joby, Wes and Anne managed to lift her father on to the mule. Anne rode the horse and Wes ran in his customary long-legged loping style, setting the pace for the animals behind. They were less than a mile from the cabin, the distance was covered in a few minutes.

Wes's concern for the safety of Gil and Alice had been lightened earlier when Anne had escaped. Johnny Stoltz had been ready to forget about Anne, to revert instead to their original plan and pass off Alice as Joby's daughter. That boded well for Alice's safety: at least she had not been killed; however, the same guarantee couldn't be given for Gil. Anne spoke up, announcing that she was prepared to return with him and help carry out any rescue plan he might be considering. Wes rejected the offer. He knew Anne's thoughts were centred on Gil Forbes and understood her desire to help, but he worked best alone. He didn't want the added worry of another person's safety, which he would have if Anne Cowell rode with him. Besides, he didn't have a plan at the moment, he wouldn't have one until he knew what had happened to Gil and Alice while he'd been away.

'Your place is here with your father,' he told her. 'He plans to move out with his gold as soon as possible and he'll need you with him.' Anne's face bore a stoic expression but it didn't fool Wes. 'Gil might not be fit enough to travel back to Council Bluffs,' he said. 'I might have to bring him here to be nursed awhile.'

Anne nodded. 'Do that, Mr Gray.'

★ ★ ★

To all intents and purposes, Wes Gray's mission on behalf of Joby Patton was finished. He'd got his daughter to him; what they now did and where they now went were not his concern. In effect he was free to return to Council Bluffs and head west with the wagon train led by Caleb Dodge. But as he made the return journey to the spot where Gil and Alice were being held captive he knew that he wouldn't cease his fight against this robber gang until all of them were punished. And he had the $200 for his pelts.

As he rode, he hoped the interpretation he'd put on Johnny Stoltz's earlier words was correct, that no harm had befallen Alice Spencer, nor, indeed, Gil Forbes, but he was well aware that unfortunate things happened to people who found themselves in the hands of desperadoes. He remembered that Alice's husband, too, was being held prisoner in Council Bluffs. If he rescued Alice he would be compelled to do the same for her husband, for his captors were members of the same gang. Finding the leader of that gang was of paramount importance to make the trail around Council Bluffs safe for prospectors and traders to travel.

Wes pulled off the trail when he was yet half a mile from his destination, worked his way swiftly and silently to the same vantage point from which he'd watched Frank Morphy and Alice earlier that morning. Gil Forbes lay at the base of a big boulder, his head in shade, his feet in sunshine. Alice Spencer sat at his feet, her arms encircling her knees, the same pose she'd adopted when waiting with Frank. Her head rested on her knees, turned so that Wes could see her face, could see the care and worry expressed upon it.

Wes Gray was able to see her face but her captors couldn't: they were beyond her, huddled together in conversation. It wasn't possible to hear their words but their movements displayed agitation, as though they were impatient for action. Judging by the number of times their attention was focused on the uphill trail, Wes was ready to assume they were anxious for the return of Johnny and Frank. Their wait would be long.

Wes picked up a small stone and lobbed it across the clearing towards Alice. It landed almost silently near her feet, disturbing a little dust as it bounced, then lay still. It caused Alice to frown and raise her head. Its arrival registered with no one else. Wes parted the branches of the brush that obscured him, showing his face to Alice. Her eyes widened and he saw her lips move. For a moment he thought Gil moved, his shoulders beginning to rise from the ground, and it was confirmed when his head turned towards the greenery where Wes waited.

It had been Wes's intention to alert Alice to his presence, to prepare her for seeking cover if a gunfight ensued, and he was heartened by her appearance, which seemed to indicate that she had not been subjected to any molestation. The fact that Gil seemed much improved was a bonus he hadn't anticipated. With the faces of the robbers still turned away from him, Wes stepped forward. Despite being a heavy man, his tread was as light as falling snow on a grizzly's coat. He moved forward six paces, stopped and waited for the men to see him.

Their surprise produced almost comical reactions. Jaws dropped open, eyes widened and each man took small, faltering, backward steps. What neither man did was reach for his gun, which showed good sense because Wes's was cocked and aimed in their direction.

'Johnny and Frank are dead,' Wes said. 'Do anything silly and you'll be dead, too.'

Neither man spoke. At Wes's signal they dropped their gunbelts and stepped away from them; then, at another signal seated themselves opposite Gil and Alice, separated by fifteen yards. Wes collected the guns and took them to where Gil lay. Satisfied that neither Gil nor Alice had suffered during their captivity, Wes was surprised when Alice spoke in defence of their guards.

'I don't think they want to be here any more than we do,' she said.

One of them spoke up. 'We took jobs on the farm,' he said. 'The foreman sent us out with Johnny Stoltz. We don't know what this is all about.'

'Were you with the gang that ambushed me on the river?'

They threw startled looks at each other. 'No, mister. Like I told you, me and Ben just work on the farm. We're heading west, took the jobs to put a few bucks in our pockets.'

'A few bucks and other people's gold.'

It was Ben who responded to Wes's goading. 'You've got it wrong. We ain't robbers. Steve told you the truth. We were sent here by the foreman. We hadn't laid eyes on that Frank fella until this morning.'

Wes was inclined to believe them but

he ordered them to turn out their pockets. If they were carrying more than a few coins he'd know they were liars, would assume any bundle of money was their share in the sale of his pelts and he would kill them; but he found only a collection of nickels, dimes and quarters. He let them put them back in their pockets.

Alice tugged at Wes's sleeve. 'The farm where they work,' she said, 'that's where Henry and I were taken when we were kidnapped. I saw that one,' she pointed at Steve, 'coming out of a barn when we got there.'

'Is Henry still there?'

Alice nodded, but because blankets had covered their heads until they got to the farm she could give no particulars of its location. 'I'd guess it was about five miles outside Council Bluffs.'

Steve spoke, nervous now at talk of kidnap, insisting that he and Ben did nothing more than odd jobs around the farm.

After a moment of thought Wes offered them a bargain. 'Give me some information and I'll let you ride clear of this territory.'

'What information?' asked Steve.

'The name of your boss.'

'I've no idea,' Steve replied. 'Never saw him. We signed on with the foreman and took our orders from him.'

'OK, the name of the foreman and the name of the farm.'

Steve and Ben exchanged glances, as though divulging the names would be a betrayal that they could barely live with. Then Ben gave a brief nod.

'Chuck Bodine's the foreman,' said Steve.

That name didn't come as a surprise. Wes remembered the brawl they had had in the livery stable, recalled the last look they'd exchanged before Bodine had pushed through the batwing doors of the saloon and the promise in that look that their dispute wasn't concluded. Bodine had been evasive when answering Sheriff Beddow's questions, had shown a raw bravado in his own defence, but that didn't make him a leader of men and Wes was sure that someone else had to be the boss of the gang.

'Where is the farm?' he asked. 'And how many men are there?'

Steve, who seemed to be the talkative one of the pair, supplied the information.

'There's a man called Carson with Bodine. We don't know anything about him. He turned up a few days ago with his arm in a sling.'

'He won't be much help around a farm,' said Wes.

'None of them were. Ben and I did all the jobs. Not exactly farm work, either. We mended a few fences and slapped whitewash on some outbuildings, but most of the time we just prepared meals and took care of the horses.'

'And the farm,' persisted Wes, 'did it have a name?'

'At one time I heard it referred to as

the Jenner place but I had a feeling that was a former owner, not the present one.'

Satisfied that the two men had no more information to impart, Wes turned his attention to his friend. Gil Forbes insisted that he was able to ride a horse, told Wes that continuing to play the invalid had been a ruse to keep Alice close to him in case their captors decided they needed some amusement, but, in verification of Alice's earlier remark, he added that neither Ben nor Steve had threatened them in any way.

Wes's and Gil's weapons formed a small pile at the foot of a tree near where the horses had been picketed. With his own gunbelt around his waist and his Bowie knife back in its sheath Wes helped Gil on to a horse. Still wearing the odd assortment of over-sized clothes, Alice seemed to be smaller and more forlorn than when they'd started on the journey. He helped her into the saddle before climbing on to a horse himself. Leading the remaining horses, he approached Steve and Ben.

'Don't go back to Council Bluffs,' he told them. 'If I see you there I'll kill you. Go south.' He pointed uphill. 'The other side leads down to the Platte and the Oregon Trail. Lots of people heading west use that.' He began to lead out.

'What about our horses?' asked Ben.

'I'm taking them with me so that you don't get any foolish ideas. Wait here an hour and you'll find them with your guns about a mile ahead.' He clucked at the horse and rode at a trot up the trail.

True to his word, he picketed two horses more than halfway through the ravine. The gunbelts he fastened and dropped over the shaft of the lance that protruded from Johnny Stoltz's body. Warning enough, he figured, to destroy any lingering thoughts of returning to Council Bluffs that Steve and Ben might harbour.

★ ★ ★

Joby Patton wasn't pleased when Wes Gray returned to his cabin. The place had been his hideaway, a jealously guarded secret which he still didn't wish to share. He was wary of all strangers and the fact that Gil Forbes was wounded and Alice Spencer was anxious to return to Council Bluffs to instigate the rescue of her husband had little impact on his attitude. Despite his broken leg, he seemed prepared to fight to deny them admittance.

Anne, however, took charge, overriding her father's complaints by ignoring them and ushering Alice and Gil inside. The ride had not been easy for Gil, but hot coffee and Anne's concern helped ease the pain.

Wes Gray had planned to set out immediately for Council Bluffs. There would be daylight for two more hours, time he could use to complete part of the downhill trip. Travelling alone, he'd be able to cover the distance in less than a day. He could be back in town by midday.

Alice Spencer, however, had other ideas. 'I'm going with you,' she told him when he announced his intention. 'My husband is being held prisoner. I've got to go. I've got to help find him.'

Other than emphasizing that he would travel faster alone, Wes had no other argument. Because neither Joby nor Gil was yet fit to ride there was no one to accompany her back to Council Bluffs if he raced ahead. Indeed, Joby had no intention of ever going back to Council Bluffs and announced that he and Anne were going over the hills to the Oregon Trail and west to Fort Laramie. The government had an assay office there and a telegraph line. When the quality of his gold was confirmed he would notify suitable consortiums, probably sell them the land so that the gold could be mined in a proper manner. He had neither the capital to instigate such a venture nor the technical know-how to achieve it. He and his daughter would move to one of the great cities and live in splendour for the rest of their lives.

Wes proposed an amendment to the first part of that plan. 'Wait here a few days until Gil is able to travel. Take him with you and join up with Caleb Dodge's wagon train. I'll explain to Caleb what's happened. He'll be happy to get his second-in-command back and you and Anne will have company all the way to Laramie.'

As was his wont, Joby grumbled, treating Wes's suggestion with suspicion, as though the frontiersman might be hatching some scheme to get the gold for himself, but Anne was in favour. The look she exchanged with Gil Forbes told Wes that they would both be happy to spend time in company with each other.

So, because there was no alternative, Alice Spencer would ride to Council Bluffs with Wes. The previous three days, however, had been a fraught experience for the girl and no matter how much she denied it, it was clear to everyone that she was exhausted. Reluctantly, Wes delayed their departure until early next morning.

12

Constrained by Alice Spencer's limitations as a horsewoman, the journey back to Council Bluffs took longer than Wes Gray had anticipated. They had left Joby's cabin at first light and it was almost dusk when they rode their overworked horses along the town's main street. Although she had voiced no complaint during the ride, when they hitched their mounts outside Sheriff Beddow's office the strain and pain of another long day in the saddle was clearly etched on Alice's face. But she dismounted without assistance, stepped quickly up on to the boardwalk and pushed open the lawman's door ahead of her companion.

Throughout his life Wes Gray had settled his own disputes, had met challenges head-on, fought his own fights and exacted his own retribution, no matter how long he had to wait, so it was against his normal mode of behaviour to seek the aide of the law. On this occasion, however, in the hope of being able to alleviate Alice Spencer's concern for her husband more quickly, he had chosen to include the sheriff in the hunt for her missing husband. Wes and Alice had spoken little on the trail but what questions he had posed had provided few details about the layout of the farm or, indeed, its actual location.

Wes had known Tom Beddow for several years, which gave him reason to believe that the lawman would accept his story and respond immediately. Also, if Alice's husband had been discovered during the last three days, Tom would be aware of the fact and might already have apprehended his kidnappers. Wes deemed that unlikely: so far the robbers had been well organised and had gone about their business undetected; there was little reason to expect anything different now.

Tom Beddow was slouched over his desk where a small lamp burned. He raised his head, the pencil in his hand lifted from the paper before him as he peered at the dust-covered couple. 'Wes,' he said. 'When did you get back?'

'Just now. Tom, this is Alice Spencer. She's the wife of Michael Riordan's missing actor. She has a story to tell you.'

'The Jenner farm,' Tom echoed when Alice and Wes had explained the situation. 'No one's lived there for two years. Hank Jenner's widow tried to keep the place going for a while after his death but it was too much for her and not making enough profit for her to hire help. She moved away. Last time I was out that way was at the end of winter. The place has fallen into disrepair and I haven't heard of anyone being interested in buying it.'

'Alice spoke of a barn near the house,' Wes pressed. 'Does that fit the layout of the farm?'

'Sure,' said Tom Beddow, 'what farm

doesn't have a barn? Stables, too.' He rubbed his jaw. 'Tell you who'll know if anyone's staying out there. Clem McGann.'

'At the assay office?'

'It's land registry, too. I reckon he'll know if someone's taken over the Jenner place.' He moved across to the window and drew the curtain aside. 'No light in his office,' he declared. 'He has living quarters behind. We'll try there.'

Wes proposed finding a room first for Alice, somewhere to rest while they tried to find her husband. Alice protested, desperate to assist in any way possible, but finally accepted that she was too weary to continue if the hunt included climbing on to another horse. That, of course, was inevitable as the Jenner farm was known to be at least five miles beyond the town limits.

'I won't sleep,' she insisted, although the darkness around her eyes seemed to tell a different story.

Wes had another concern. Although it was a slim chance, because she had been seen little in the town before her kidnap, he didn't want anyone to recognize her, didn't want any other member of the gang to know that she had returned. Her presence in Council Bluffs would be evidence that their plan had failed, and a new search for her husband would be under way.

Tom Beddow suggested she remain in the jail. 'The bunks aren't comfortable,' he told her, 'but no one will disturb you while we're gone.'

Leaving Alice with coffee, blankets and the door key, Wes and Tom went in search of Clem McGann. His office was locked and they could get no answer to their knocking on the door to his living quarters. The sheriff suggested the Long Lariat saloon. 'Clem's been known to get involved in poker games there,' he explained, and his hunch was right. The tall government man was facing the door when they entered, occupying a round table with three others. A small collection of bills and coins sat on the table in front of them and cards were held possessively in their hands.

Clem looked up as they entered, seemed to fix his attention on them as if knowing they had come for him, but Tom allowed the hand to be played out before beckoning him to join them at the bar. Clem spoke ruminatively when responding to the sheriff's enquiry, his fingers idling with his whiskey shot glass. 'No, no one has shown any interest in the Jenner place.'

'Have you been out there recently?'

Clem McGann shook his head. 'I've got no reason to visit. I just register the transfer of deeds.' He paused a moment, scratched at his jaw like a man in deep thought. 'Try Abe Cotton. I believe he represented Mrs Jenner when she sold up. No doubt he's handling the sale of the farm on her behalf. Talk to him, he'll know if anyone is staying there.'

Abe Cotton, Tom Beddow explained when he and Wes were back on the street, was the oldest-established lawyer in Council Bluffs. 'Abe's semi-retired now,' he added. 'Doesn't take new clients. He lives beyond the south meadow where the westbound wagons congregate.'

'How far?'

'Three miles.'

Wes wondered if there was anything to be gained by riding out there, but Tom Beddow said that another hour wasn't likely to be critical. If Henry Spencer wasn't already dead there was no reason to suppose he would be killed during the time it would take to get to the Cotton place and back. 'Better to gather all the knowledge we can before making our strike,' he argued.

It wasn't Wes's way; he was in favour of storming the farm as soon as possible; what did it matter who now occupied the Jenner place? If Henry Spencer was being held there then it was only right to free him as soon as possible. But he'd involved the law and now he figured that he had to be guided by it. Tom Beddow, he suspected, being a careful man, applied his own methods to the job so that he ensured equal treatment for all when maintaining law and order. If he chose to gather facts before taking action then Wes would bridle his own impatience and let the lawman lead the way. Besides, passing the wagon train gave him the opportunity to stop off and tell Caleb Dodge about Gil Forbes's injury and the need of Joby Patton and his daughter to travel with the wagon train as far as Fort Laramie.

'And how am I going to get everyone as far as the Blue without my right-hand man?' spluttered Caleb when he heard the news.

Wes had absolute faith in the wagon master to get his charges all the way to California on his own if it proved necessary, but he humoured Caleb's grumpiness.

'I'll be with you,' he said. 'We'll manage.'

'You? Yes, you'll be with me if you don't go off and get yourself killed chasing robbers who are none of your business.'

'That's not my intention.' Wes's voice carried a coldness that was capable of unsettling even his friend Caleb Dodge.

'No,' said the wagon master, 'I don't suppose it is.'

* * *

Abe Cotton was surprised not only by the arrival of the sheriff at that late hour, but also by the purpose of his visit.

'I didn't handle Mrs Jenner's legal affairs,' he told Tom and Wes. 'Can't think why Clem McGann would say I did. Hank Jenner made his opinion of me well known in town when he lost that boundary dispute during his first year here. He never spoke to me again. I'm surprised you don't know that yourself, Sheriff. Clem McGann certainly does.'

Mounted again, Tom Beddow expressed his anger at the wasted

journey and turned his horse to the trail back to Council Bluffs, but it was Wes Gray who sensed something more sinister. He pointed out that sending them south seemed almost like a deliberate manoeuvre on the part of Clem McGann, an attempt to keep them away from the Jenner farm, which was north-east of the town, miles away in the opposite direction.

'I think we should get to the Jenner farm as quickly as possible,' he said.

By retracing their steps and following the recognized trail, the ride ahead of them would be at least thirty minutes. Tom Beddow knew of another route, one which would save them several minutes. A short distance from Abe Cotton's home they took advantage of a ford and crossed the river to the flat grassland of the far bank. Here, no established trail existed, no twists for the observance of man-made boundaries that added distance to the journey, and at this side of the river, too, they avoided both the township of Council Bluffs and the wagon encampment. Wes and Tom gave their horses their heads, allowed them to race unchecked across the meadow and were soon recrossing the river at another suitable point north of town.

Above the river, on a small plateau that, even by moonlight, gave them a panoramic view, albeit in black-and-purple silhouette, they halted so that Tom Beddow could get his bearings. He pointed to the east.

'About a mile,' he stated, even though Wes hadn't asked how much further ahead the Jenner place lay. 'The road to town passes the other side of that coppice and the trail to the farm forks off there.'

They rode on, choosing a small hillock at the rear from which to study the farm.

'How are we going to handle this?' asked Wes. 'You just going to ride up to the door and demand admittance?'

'That's pretty much it,' Tom Beddow

told him. 'We don't know that there is anyone there.'

'If there isn't it means they've already killed Alice's husband.'

'I'm the sheriff,' said Tom. 'I've got to give them the chance to tell their story.'

'More likely they'll just shoot you out the saddle,' Wes told him.

'Chance I've got to take. I'll have my rifle in my hands.'

Wes removed his hat and with the same arm wiped his brow. He wasn't sweating, simply giving himself a moment before making a suggestion.

'I could take a look around first,' he said. 'See how many people are there and if there's any sign of the actor.'

'If you get caught they might shoot you for trespassing.'

Even the night couldn't hide Wes Gray's grin from Tom Beddow, nor obscure the frontiersman's certainty that he wouldn't be caught.

'Before you came here you rode out to Abe Cotton's place to learn what he knew. Seems to me that if you're that careful you might as well wait a few more minutes while I check over the place.'

The sheriff stiffened at the other's words, sensing a criticism of his earlier caution, but Tom Beddow was a good lawman, not one to dismiss a good idea because of a personal slight.

'OK,' he said, 'we'll ride down to the boundary fence and you can have ten minutes to look around the place.'

Wes descended with no more sound than that of a cougar on the prowl. He rolled under the bottom bar of the fence, then, in a crouched run, reached the rear wall of one of the outbuildings: the barn, he guessed, where Steve had been seen by Alice Spencer.

He made his way along the side of the barn, paused at the corner and looked across the yard to the house. Somewhere a shutter clattered as it was shifted by the breeze, but that seemed to add to the sense of desolation, abandonment, rather than imply habitation. He paused a moment, listening for other sounds and scanning the night for a sign of human presence, but it was his nose that provided the first clue. Horses; the distinct smell of a recently run horse hung in the air. Gently he edged open the barn door.

Two stalls were occupied, the beasts turning their heads with quiet interest. In here there was no aroma of fresh horse sweat and Wes ran a hand down their flanks to confirm that these horses had not been run recently. He found two saddles hoisted over a rack near the door. If Steve and Ben had told the truth then Wes had to assume that these belonged to Chuck Bodine and the man called Carson. Wes closed the door behind him and slipped back out into the night.

He found a team of recently run horses on the far side of the house. They were harnessed to a buggy and tethered to a rail under an old oak tree. Two bags were tied to the back of the buggy, suggesting that someone was about to make a long trip. Wes checked them but they were locked and he didn't propose wasting time finding out who they belonged to, although he believed he already knew the man's identity: Clem McGann, who, apart from Tom Beddow and Caleb Dodge, was the only one in Council Bluffs who knew that the girl for whom Wes had been searching was Joby Patton's daughter. He was also the one man who had any knowledge of the true worth of Joby's strike. When Wes walked into the Long Lariat he must have known that his plan had failed and that discovery of his crimes was imminent. He'd sent Wes and the sheriff off on a wild-goose chase to give himself time to escape the clutches of the law. Tom's knowledge of the territory meant that that plan was about to fail, too.

From within, the drawn curtains of the nearest room were illuminated by lamp-glow. The sound of a chair scraping across the floor carried to Wes and he figured he'd arrived without a minute to spare. If Henry Spencer was still alive it was essential to find him without delay. Wes thought of Tom Beddow. He would be anxious now for his return and Wes wondered how strictly he would adhere to the ten-minute deadline he'd set. Raised voices and the clumsy noises of a brief scuffle came from within. Wes decided he needed to act immediately.

Above him, in irregular fashion, with a motion governed by the variable strength of the breeze, swung the shutter making the noise he'd heard from the barn. Sometimes it struck the frame of a partly opened upstairs window. Repairing it, Wes reckoned, was a job that Steve and Ben hadn't had time to complete, and they wouldn't be back to fix it now. He examined the tree under which he now stood, noted how a branch reached close to that window and instantly, with agility, scaled the oak.

It took little more than a cursory inspection of the sash frame to know that he wouldn't be able to open the window any wider without using considerable force and making a proportionate amount of noise, but Wes wasn't prepared to forsake the opportunity to attack his enemies from an unexpected quarter. Commanding the high ground was always an advantage in battle and he had no reason to deem it otherwise on this occasion.

The available gap was less than two feet high but Wes slithered through into the dark room beyond. He paused only long enough to allow his eyes to become accustomed to the dimmer light, and to listen for sounds beyond the room which might be a telltale sign that his entrance had disturbed the current occupants of the building. Satisfied that he had not been detected, he opened the door. Voices rose from below, not raised and angry but also not without a certain tension, an underlying disagreement that could, at any minute, develop into an argument. Keeping to the available shadowed niches of the corridor, Wes made his way to the top of the stairs which led down to a long, lamplit room: the one, he figured, that he'd stood outside before climbing the oak tree.

Clem McGann was on one knee packing saddle-bags with bundles of paper money from a squat iron safe which stood in one corner of the room.

'If I was you,' he said, throwing the words over his shoulder before returning his concentration to the contents of the safe, 'I'd put miles behind you before Tom Beddow gets here.' He stood up, threw one of the bundles of banknotes to Chuck Bodine, together with a gesture that the money was to be shared with his companion. 'The sheriff's got that half-Indian fellow with him. He's already put a slug in your shoulder, Carson, and he was close to cutting your heart out,' he told Bodine, words which were meant to humiliate his henchmen and hurry them on their way without quarrelling about the diminutive share he'd doled out to them.

'And what about him?' Bodine inclined his head towards the fourth man in the room, a grey-faced, fair-haired man, bound hand and foot, half-sitting, half-lying, slouched on a long, stuffed and backless seat at the opposite end of the room.

'Take him with you,' said McGann. 'Get rid of him somewhere along the trail. Make sure there's no trace of him left here.' He walked across the room, looked down on the prisoner. 'Pity,' he said. 'I've always enjoyed the work of Shakespeare. I'm sure that you and your wife would have performed the scenes with great skill. Tragedy, I believe, is your forte. How fitting.'

Clem McGann began to head for the door, at which moment Wes Gray, gun in hand, chose to step out of the shadows at the head of the stairs. It was Carson who first saw the frontiersman descend. His first instinct was to make a move for his gun, his torso twisting towards the stairs and his right shoulder beginning to roll to accommodate the necessary arm and hand movements for drawing and firing his weapon. But the movement never developed. Carson's right arm was still bound up in a sling; grasping a weapon was prohibited to him.

The resulting grunt, however, which combined surprise at the appearance of the frontiersman and frustration that the injury rendered him defenceless, also acted as a warning to Chuck Bodine. Bodine turned in the direction of Carson's gaze and swore when he recognized the intruder. His instinct, too, was to go for his gun, but he was sensible enough to know that he had no chance against Wes Gray, whose gun was already held firmly in his hand.

At that moment, a voice hailed the house. 'This is Sheriff Beddow.'

Clem McGann, still unaware of Wes Gray's presence, reacted like a hair-trigger, sweeping aside a nearby lamp with the saddle-bags he carried, putting that part of the room into darkness. Wes fired at the government man but the bullet thudded harmlessly into the wall. Taking advantage of Wes's distraction, Chuck Bodine followed his leader's example and extinguished the other lamp, plunging the room into darkness. He drew his gun and fired three shots up the stairway, disappointed not to hear at least a groan to signify the mark had been hit by at least one of the bullets.

Wes Gray's reactions were no less sharp than those of his opponents. When Chuck Bodine swept aside the lamp Wes leapt over the side-rail, soundlessly dropping on to the balls of his moccasin-clad feet. Crouching behind the staircase, he waited for someone to reveal their location. Tom Beddow shouted again, repeating the fact that he was the sheriff and telling those inside to cease fire. Wes hoped he wouldn't be foolish enough to enter the house for he'd make an easy target as a silhouette in the doorway.

Then Wes felt a draught on the back of his neck. He glanced that way and it seemed to him that there was movement at that window. Although he'd last seen Clem McGann at that side of the room, Wes didn't fire. There was a chance that Tom Beddow had worked his way to that side of the building and was trying to find an alternative entry point. Wes didn't want to accidently shoot the lawman. Flat on the floor, squirming snakelike, he made his way across the room.

A noise sounded from the other side of the room, whispering: Bodine and Carson were hatching a plan. It was clear that they didn't relish hunting for Wes Gray in the dark, even in the confined space of one room. It had been Bodine who had put the room into darkness, believing in that first instance that one of the three shots he'd fired would kill or disable the man. Now, however, it was apparent that Wes Gray was unharmed and hunting them.

'Get the actor,' Bodine whispered to Carson. 'He'll get us out of here.'

Carson wasn't in a hurry to comply.

Moving across the room was likely to draw Wes Gray's fire, but there was nothing to be gained by standing still. Outside, an exchange of gunshots sounded. A horse nickered, too, and Carson, either jerked into action by the noises or believing that they would distract Wes Gray, plunged through the darkness towards the long seat on which Henry Spencer lay. Reaching down with his one good hand he grabbed a handful of clothing and hauled the man to his feet. It was the ease with which the man arose that triggered the first suspicion in Carson's mind, followed swiftly by the fact that the material in his hand was not the linen shirt that Henry Spencer wore, but a buckskin jacket.

'Bodine,' he croaked, 'it's Gray.'

Wes Gray was turning Carson even as he spoke, gripping his neck in the crook of his left arm, nudging him, forcing him to walk towards Bodine.

Bodine, alarmed by the fear in Carson's voice, didn't hesitate. He fired, once, twice, both slugs thumping into Carson, whose body was acting as a shield for Wes Gray. Carson's weight was almost too much for Wes to hold as the dying body staggered backwards, but it didn't prevent Wes Gray from firing two shots at the flares from Bodine's six-shooter. Across the room he heard the crash as Chuck Bodine's body fell against a small table, then on to the floor.

'I'll be back,' Wes told the still-bound actor, whom he'd pulled on to the floor when replacing him on the seat.

He opened the door slowly. A voice called, 'This is the sheriff. Come out with your hands up.'

'Hold your fire, Tom. It's Wes Gray.'

Wes was relieved that the sheriff wasn't injured and happier yet to see Clem McGann grimacing with pain on the high seat of the two-horse buggy. There were handcuffs on his wrists and the growing dark stain on his left shoulder indicated that he was losing blood quickly.

★　★　★

Clem McGann died from the wound he'd received during the exchange of gunfire with Tom Beddow but not before the sheriff had uncovered sufficient evidence of the assayer's involvement with the attacks on the prospectors. It came to light during those investigations that Clem McGann owned the farm where Henry Spencer had been held captive, having paid Mrs Jenner less than ten cents on the dollar of its true worth. His purpose for buying the land was unknown, Tom Beddow drawing the conclusion that McGann was so confident that his involvement with the robberies would never be suspected that he intended to settle permanently in Council Bluffs.

Wes Gray felt that he had been cheated when he was told of McGann's death. From the combined pockets of Johnny Stoltz, Chuck Bodine and Carson he had garnered little more than half of the $200 that Ezzie Temple had paid for the pelts. Even taking into consideration the horse and rifle he'd used to barter with Ezzie and Luke Brandon, he was out of pocket and Tom Beddow had refused outright to furnish the difference from the banknotes in Clem McGann's saddle-bags. The loss angered Wes, not because money ruled his thoughts but because there was no justice in the loss. It was his creed that what he'd earned was his to keep.

Henry and Alice Spencer appeared only once at Michael Riordan's theatre in Council Bluffs. They were treated to a great ovation, earned for the most part by the reputation which had brought them to town in the first place, and increased by the knowledge of their recent misadventure. Their tribulations at the hands of Clem McGann and his gang must surely have affected their performance, but whether for good or bad no one could say, for no one in the audience had seen them on stage prior to that night, although other, less celebrated actors had presented Shakespeare's soliloquies before them.

The guest of honour, Wes Gray, whose previous knowledge of theatre acts consisted of loud, brassy music and big, colourful girls, relied on Major Caleb Dodge to lavish praise on the Spencers after the show, which the wagon master, showing rare gregariousness, was happy to do.

Two days later he started the wagons on their westbound trek. Wes Gray was at his side, fulfilling the role that truly belonged to Gil Forbes and which meant that he was tied to the wagons for two weeks. They would meet up with Gil and Joby Patton and his daughter at the Blue River, and that day couldn't come soon enough for Wes. Then he would be released from the constraints of the wagon train and he would be alone again, depending upon no one and nothing, content to live in the manner of the tribespeople. Until they reached California where, for a short while he would be forced to endure the conventions of civilization, he would cease to think of himself as Wes Gray. Once again he would be Medicine Feather, brother of the Arapaho, friend of the Sioux.